'Tis the season for secrets…

and for true love.

Yuletide Lies

by Susan Gee Heino

Dedication

For all those who've ever selflessly shared their life
with a creature who could give nothing back
but pure, unconditional love.

It was well worth the effort, wasn't it?

Chapter 1

The Midlands, England, 1814

Being cold to the bone had never been one of Cassandra's favorite conditions. Being cold and wet was even lower on her list of preferred circumstances. Today, however, had brought a new element. Today she was cold, wet and quite terrified on top of it all. This was, by far, the most awful state she had ever found herself in.

And things seemed to be getting worse.

"Please make the man drive more slowly!" she begged, although Papa was doing his best to pretend he was asleep and therefore immune to her distress.

Mr. Rovish, however, was not sleeping. He leaned forward in his seat and smiled at her. The frantic jostling of the rickety carriage on this abysmal excuse for a road seemed to have no ill effect on him. But then again, Mr. Rovish was so vile, so thoroughly abysmal himself that it seemed entirely possible the man's constitution might thrive on this discomfort that they'd been enduring for the past many hours.

How many hours she truly had no clue. Their journey so far had seemed endless.

"Is the delicate lady concerned for her safety?" he

asked, although his tone sounded anything but concerned.

"I fear I shall be covered in bruises by the time we get wherever it is we are going," she said sharply, hoping perhaps Papa might hear her and put his head up just long enough to order their driver to take more care for his passengers.

If the driver would, indeed, take orders from Papa. Early on Papa had told her he was in charge of this ill-conceived venture, but as the day had gone on she'd begun to wonder at that. It was beginning to seem Papa had little to say about things and Mr. Rovish held sway of their plans and their perilous speed. Cassandra did not like it any one bit.

If Papa had confessed to her what they were about when he convinced her—by falsehood, as usual—to trust him, she'd never have allowed herself to get pulled into this scheme. Heavens, what on earth good could come out of this? Papa was a fool and Grandmother must be worried sick by now. It was cruel what Papa and Mr. Rovish had planned even if they did assure her that no one would suffer. After hours and hours in this carriage, she was most definitely suffering and it was becoming clear no one cared in the least.

Once again she'd let herself believe her father was capable of warm, parental feelings for her and now look where it had gotten her. Miles away from home and utterly wretched. She supposed she deserved all this misery for being such a fool.

"Would the lady prefer a more comfortable seat?" Mr. Rovish said, his voice oily and low. "Come sit yourself over here. I'll make you quite comfortable."

She did not bother to honor his disgusting offer with

a reply. No doubt the sickened expression on her face would be enough to let him know just what she thought of that suggestion. The man was a beast. How on earth could Papa consider him his friend? Had the misguided old man truly sunk so low as this? Then what did that say of her?

Nothing good, obviously, for here she was with him. Unwilling, perhaps, but here she was, a participant in this hateful plot. And just days before Christmas! She should have never let things go this far, should have called for help at the inn where they stopped to get a quick meal and trade out the horse.

But of course she hadn't. For Papa's sake, she'd kept quiet and done just as she'd been told. She'd acted her part and let the innkeeper catch a glimpse of her, just enough to be memorable.

As per Papa's terrible plan, Grandmother would no doubt send men out to hunt for her. After all, what would make the dear woman suspicious that the note she received saying Cassandra was kidnapped could have possibly come from Papa? Grandmother's search party would only discover witnesses who had seen her in company of two disreputable looking men. Grandmother would never guess it was all a ruse. She'd pay the ransom as ordered and call it a miracle when Cassandra was safely returned. Papa and his crony would pocket the money and expect Cassandra to keep quiet or risk seeing Papa tossed into jail. It was awful and unfair.

Drat the horrible Mr. Rovish! She knew it all had to be his doing. Papa was content to spend his days with the bottle; he would hardly have gone to all the trouble to think this scheme up on his own. Shame on him—

and on her as well—for falling into Mr. Rovish's clutches to be used in such a manner. Of course Grandmother could easily afford the ransom Papa said they would demand, but this whole thing was very, very wrong.

And she was beginning to fear she ought not trust that Mr. Rovish would allow it to end as it was designed. The way he eyed her from across the dim carriage seats... oh, but she hated him. Just what, exactly, *did* he have in mind for her aside from his hopes for ill-gotten gain?

Perhaps it would be best if she did not contemplate that. Oh, but if only Papa would stand up to the man, would do something to convince her he was still in control and she would end up safely returned to Grandmother once their dratted ransom was paid! But Papa made no move, uttered no sound. His head lolled against the worn leather of the thin padding along the carriage wall.

How could he sleep at a time like this? Infuriating man! She should never have let silly sentiment warm her toward him. Papa had always been a useless dreg, ever since the day Mamma went to her reward and left a very young Cassandra alone with him. Heavens, she shuddered to think what might have come of her if Grandmother hadn't tracked them down and taken her back to live at Wythelea Abby.

In all honesty, though, she had to admit she'd probably have ended up just about where she was now. It was a very bleak realization.

"Wake up, Papa," she said when she could take no more of Mr. Rovish's leering. "Surely we must be nearing our destination. It will be night soon and I

cannot imagine you expect to travel these wintry roads after dark."

He still slumbered away, despite the ferocious jostling of the carriage. Oh, but the old fool must be drunk. She'd seen him nipping from the flask he thought he'd concealed so cleverly in his ill-fitting coat. How could he do that, drink himself into oblivion while she was trapped here with the lusty eyed Mr. Rovish? This venture just got worse and worse and she would have kicked herself if she could.

As it was, however, she thought it might be best to save any violent efforts for Mr. Rovish. He was still sneering at her and leaning forward in his seat. She recoiled from his polluted breath when he spoke.

"It appears your dear father is rather dead to the world, my dear Miss Loring."

Even the man's laughter was foul.

She nudged Papa with an elbow. "Papa, look out the window and tell me where we are."

"We are nowhere," Mr. Rovish answered for him. "Nowhere at all, I'm afraid."

"We have to be *somewhere*," she corrected. "Papa instructed the driver and no doubt he'll know where we are."

She nudged him again, none too gently. His head rolled on his shoulders, his chin coming to rest on his chest but his eyes remained closed and he made no response to her nudging. She tried even harder, then patted his cheek. It was then she noticed the unthinkable.

He was cold! Good lord, but she shook him in desperation. His head banged against the carriage sides, but he was no closer to waking than he had been. His eyes did slide open just a bit, however. They were glassy and dull.

Dear God! She pulled away from him, plastering herself against the far side of their seat. Papa just sat there, his spare flesh sagging with the motion of the carriage and his eyes glaring with unseeing persistence. His head tipped at a cock-eyed angle and the corner of his lips drooped slightly open.

Papa was dead.

"Why look, Miss Loring. It appears I was correct. Your father *is* dead to the world."

It was true. Papa had died on her! Now she was alone with Mr. Rovish, far, far away from everything she knew. Indeed, he had been correct on all counts. Papa was dead and she, as far as the rest of the world was concerned, truly was *nowhere*.

She took stock of her situation and did the only thing she could think of. She dove for the door.

But Mr. Rovish was quick. He grabbed her before she could make good an escape, though not before her actions had unlatched the door. It swung open, revealing a sleeting twilight landscape of windblown wilderness. They were jouncing precariously along the edge of a muddy, rock-strewn hillside. The ground beyond the carriage door fell dramatically away and Cassandra realized that had she been able to throw herself out as she'd intended, she'd most assuredly have ended up worse off than her current situation. Which was not very good.

Mr. Rovish had his greasy hands on her, pulling her up into the seat beside him and pressing her to his side. She was determined not to make things easy for him, however. She fought and kicked and then screamed when Papa's body came tipping forward into her lap. Mr. Rovish laughed, which simply proved him to be even more of a monster than she had already determined.

He booted Papa back onto the opposite seat and then pinned Cassandra against the wall, holding her there with one firm hand while the other reached into his coat. It came out with a pistol. She barely contained another scream.

"Now, my dear, if you'd be so kind as to stop this infernal struggling and simply let me have my way with you," he said.

She struggled all the more, until the pistol was pressed against her cheek.

"I *will* do as I intend," he hissed. "And I won't mind doing it when you've got a bullet in you. So you might as well give up and live a while longer. If you're a very good girl, in fact, I might let you live a long, long time."

"You wouldn't dare kill me," she said and the break in her voice gave away the full terror she felt.

"Wouldn't I?" he asked. "I had no qualms about killing your father."

"*You* did that?" She had assumed it was all the years of Papa's dissolute life that had finally caught up with him. Apparently not.

"You can't believe it's simple coincidence, can you? No, I put something into his bloody flask at our last stop. Took the stupid fool this long to finally imbibe enough to do the job, though. Apparently he thought he was hiding it from you."

He laughed again at the macabre situation. Cassandra's stomach roiled. It was bad enough to think

Papa's worthless heart had finally stopped pumping all
on its own, but to realize this was murder... What on
earth was she going to do?

"Now, let's just get this over with. Keep still if you
don't want the pistol to go off. It would be a shame to
join poor Papa in the afterlife so very quickly, wouldn't
it?"

He moved over her as if he actually expected her to
comply. Indeed she would not! An eternity spent rotting
away wherever Papa had gone seemed infinitely
preferable to whatever Mr. Rovish had planned for her.
She shut her eyes, gritted her teeth, and shoved the man
with all the force she could muster.

Apparently she had mustered quite a lot. He lost his
balance on the narrow seat and had to take the pistol
away from her face long enough to catch himself from
falling. She took advantage of this and brought her knee
up sharply, connecting with his chin. He swung
viciously at her, bringing the pistol back to aim, but she
kicked at his arm. The carriage exploded with sound.
The gun had gone off, the smell of burnt powder filled
the air and for a moment she waited to feel the searing
pain of a lead ball. But she felt nothing beyond the
jostle of the carriage and the wind howling through the
door as it slammed back and forth.

Mr. Rovish was still looming over her, though. And
laughing.

"You think your petty efforts are going to stop me?
Oh, you are quite wrong, my dear."

The spent pistol smoked in his hand, but it seemed
every bit as lethal as before. He might not be able to
shoot her just now, but clearly the man was not about to
let go of his plans. All she'd accomplished was to assure

her death would be by much slower, more painful means than gunfire.

She tried to lash out, to kick him again, but the carriage lurched and her aim was off. He laughed again, then stopped as something heavy thumped against the side of the carriage. It lurched again and she was crushed against the wall as they were thrown sideways. One of the front wheels seemed to be grinding, causing them to list dangerously close to the edge of the slick roadway. The loud thumping continued.

Mr. Rovish steadied himself and peered out the gaping door. Cassandra tried to position herself to knock him off his perch and hopefully out the door, but he was too wary for that. He held the doorframe securely and then pulled back to glare at her.

"Damn you, girl," he spat. "You made me shoot the driver!"

What? Heavens, was it true? When the gun had gone off the bullet penetrated the carriage and killed their lone driver? This was very, very bad for them!

Mr. Rovish swore. "Now the poor sap's fallen off and gotten tangled up in our wheel. I don't know how I'll—"

He didn't get to finish his words. The carriage was leaning too far. They hit a rock which bounced them both, and Mr. Rovish tumbled out the door. Cassandra didn't have time to wish him a broken neck, though, because only a few feet farther the carriage jerked sideways and followed the man right over the edge of the jagged hillside. More than a hillside, really. It could have been called, quite accurately, a cliff.

She was tossed around inside and would likely have tumbled out the open doorway herself if not for Papa's thick body landing on her and partially pinning her to the floor between the seats. She struggled to move from under him, to catch her breath, but the carriage was rolling. The horse screamed into the night and Cassandra was jumbled about. Her heart pounded and her head ached. It was impossible to tell up from down and the fall seemed to go on endlessly. She must be falling to the center of the earth.

Then suddenly all was still. Splinters of wood from broken carriage bits jabbed her. Papa's heavy arm was across her back, holding her to what was left of the leather bench. Her legs were pinned beneath broken planks. Slivers of dim, gray light filtered through the carriage windows, but it seemed she had fallen into a murky pit. The wind whistled overhead and spatters of rain trickled through the wreckage onto her. There were warmer droplets, too. Blood, perhaps.

Her head throbbed. She must have been shaken and tossed about the interior of this carriage like a rag doll. Her body would be covered in bruises. She was cold, although that hardly mattered. Darkness was closing around her and in the distance she could hear one carriage wheel squeaking as it, presumably, turned uselessly in the cold gusts. That sound was overshadowed by the pained cries of their horse. Poor thing. It had certainly done nothing to deserve such a fate. Of all of them, that poor horse was the only truly innocent victim. She would have helped him if she could.

Little chance of that, though. She could not even help herself. The darkness was closing in fast, closing in to claim her. Most likely forever.

Chapter 2

The darkness gave way to cold, gray haze. She wanted the darkness back. This haze burned her eyes, as a matter of fact. She tried to cover them, but her arms felt as if weights had been strapped to her wrists. With great effort, she finally managed to gain control of her right arm and lifted her hand to her face.

Exhausted from the effort, her arm seemed to fall from her control and flopped down onto her forehead. The pain was immediate and intense. She groaned.

"There, there, little miss," a stranger's voice soothed. "Lie still and I'll tend ye."

She didn't much like being told what to do by a stranger. She needed to move... to get away. Yes, that's what she'd been doing. She was trying to get away... Ah yes, from Mr. Rovish. Heavens, how had she forgotten? She was trapped in the carriage with Mr. Rovish and Papa was...

The headache almost overwhelmed her. If it wasn't for that annoying grayness she would have easily slipped back into sleep. Or had she been dead? No, surely being dead could not hurt quite this much. She must still be living. If that were the case, then clearly she had to escape. If only her muscles would obey her commands! She could barely move her arm from her face enough to peer into the chilled colorless haze.

"Don't fret yourself, now," the maternal voice continued, moving closer and bringing with it the sound of water sloshing in a pan. "A cool cloth for your head will help ease the pain."

Sure enough, the voice was correct. Cassandra's arm was gently moved out of the way and replaced on her forehead by a soft, cool cloth. It was heavenly. Perhaps she was dead, after all, and her caregiver an angel.

The old woman bending over her didn't look much like an angel, however. And the gray haze turned out to be light from a cloudy morning beaming in through a window. A large, many-paned window with rich, wine colored drapery. Did heaven have drapery? Probably not draperies like these. They had tiny holes from moths chewed into them.

"Where am I?" Cassandra rasped out.

"MacMorton Castle, of course," the old woman replied, as if Cassandra should have anticipated her answer.

"But... how did I get here? I don't... I don't recall anything after the..."

Now the old woman shook her head sadly. "The carriage accident. Yes, quite a miracle you survived. His lordship said it looked... well, you are lucky he found you when he did."

"His lordship?"

"Indeed, carried you back here himself," the woman seemed quite pleased by this. "I must say, when you and your father didn't arrive here as planned, we were all a bit worried, what with the roads as they are, and all."

When they didn't arrive as planned? Good gracious, but this kindly old woman was in on the scheme! Papa

12

must have been bringing her here all along. Well, at least she could take some small consolation in knowing that he had meant to keep her safe, to bring her to someone at least partially civilized. Although, despite the woman's caring demeanor now, how civilized could she be if she'd been in league with the likes of Mr. Rovish?

"So Papa had planned to...?"

She wasn't quite certain how to phrase her question. Could she trust this woman? Was the original plan still in place, with word having been sent to Grandmother that she'd been abducted by strangers? How long would she be expected to remain here before being released and sent home? Would she be sent home? Her headache grew worse as questions bombarded her already overwhelmed brain.

"Poor little miss," the woman said, patting her and freshening the cloth. "I'm so sorry for ye. The truth is, I'm afraid you're the only one to survive that horrible wreck."

"But my father..."

She stopped short of mentioning what Mr. Rovish had done. Best to get her bearings, learn the loyalties of this woman and whoever the "lordship" person might be, before bringing up any further details.

"I'm sorry, dove. Your father... well, he's..."

"He's dead."

"Yes. God rest his soul. If it's any comfort to ye, his lordship says he seems to have gone peacefully. It must have been quick; there were no signs that he suffered."

She pinched her eyes shut and nodded. Yes, despite all the man's wrong-doing and neglect over the years, he had indeed died quite peacefully. She probably should not, considering the situation, but she did take some small comfort in that. He had gone to his maker on a full stomach and a gut sated with Rovish's ill-doctored ale.

"And what of the other man?" she asked carefully, silently praying that evidence might show Mr. Rovish had not met quite an easy end as her father.

"Other man? Oh, the driver. No, I'm very sorry, miss. He was thrown from his seat and... well, he did not make it."

"And... that is it? There was no sign of anyone... er, rather, I alone survived?"

"Tis quite a tragedy. A shock to ye, I'm sure, waking up to such a loss. Oh, there is one bit of good. I suppose it is little consolation, but the horse did survive."

"The horse?"

"His lordship is quite good with animals. No one would have thought the poor beast might survive such a tumble down that hillside, but his lordship said not to use a bullet and end his suffering. He says he can mend the creature, and I believe he'll do just that. Fine man, his lordship, if I do say so."

"And just who is his lordship, if I may ask?"

The woman laughed and tsk-ed twice. "My, but you did take a bump to that pretty head of yours. He's Lord Braden, of course. The same man you've been in correspondence with these many weeks."

She had? No, indeed she'd never heard of the man before now. Best to play along, though.

"Ah yes, Lord Braden. Of course."

So Papa must have been plotting this far longer than she'd been led to believe. How presumptuous of him to lead these people to think she had been in on the plot from the very start. Just what else had he told them of her? More important, why did the woman make no mention of Mr. Rovish? Had they not found his body?

He'd gone out of the carriage before the long tumble to the valley floor. Perhaps he had not ended up near the carriage, was still somewhere on that hillside. But of course he was dead. He must be. Surely in the light of day someone would find him, battered and torn, smashed against the rocks and left to bleed out like a stuck pig.

But what if they did not? What if somehow she had *not* been the sole survivor of the accident? If Mr. Rovish still lived and she was in the home of conspirators, then she was still very much in danger! She had to leave now.

But the room spun around as she tried to muster the will to sit up. The old woman pressed her gently back into her pillow. It felt so good to allow it, to let herself sink into the soft linens. If only she could fall back into that precious, dreamless sleep that had protected her from the pain of reality. She simply didn't dare, though.

"Now hush yourself, dear," the woman said. "You'll be whole again soon, but for now you must rest. Lord Braden will be in to see you, now that you're awake. He's been quite worried, you know."

"Worried? For me?"

This seemed amusing to her. "Indeed, for you. The poor man hasn't rested one wink since his hound alerted him to the trouble and he went out in search of you. As I said, he's a fine, fine man."

"Yes, he must be."

"He is. Now rest a bit while I go have cook make up

a tray for you. Surely you must be a bit hungry by now."

"A bit, perhaps. Thank you."

"There's a strong lass."

The woman patted her shoulder, adjusted her cloth, resituated her covers, and nodded, quite pleased. She went to the door then turned back with a motherly smile.

"You'll like it here, Miss Horne."

"Thank you, I... er, Miss Horne?"

"Just rest. After you eat we'll tidy you up so Lord Braden can see for himself that we've been taking good care of his guest."

The woman was gone into the hallway with the door shut behind her before Cassandra could at last catch her breath. What name had the woman called her? *Miss Horne?* Oh, but clearly the woman was under some grave misunderstanding!

They had not been expecting Papa at all. They'd been waiting for some other group, another set of travelers. Travelers they'd clearly not met before, but knew only from correspondence. Travelers who, given the state of the roads, were very likely considerably delayed in their journey and would not be here for some time.

Cassandra needed to think. The pounding in her head and the aches in her body made that extremely difficult, but she forced herself to put that all aside. What was important now was to determine her next step. Was it really possible that she was not in grave danger here?

If these people thought she were Miss Horne, then they could know nothing of Papa's plan, or Mr. Rovish's treachery. They would treat her as an esteemed guest. Could she dare allow them to continue in misunderstanding? If no one knew who she was, she could wait out the weather safe and secure right here in this soft bed. Indeed, as hard as she thought and the more that she contemplated, she could not come up with one single reason to support telling the truth.

Other than simple morality, of course, and just now that did not seem to matter as much as survival.

Chapter 3

Lord Braden paced nervously. His boots echoed on the polished marble of the grand entry hall. Even with the armloads of greenery that his servants had carried indoors, the place still sounded hollow and empty.

Because it *was* hollow and empty. He had long since sold the fine sculptures that had once filled niches along the wall or graced the pedestals that now sat barren in rows beside the grand staircase. He would have sold the staircase if he'd been able to, actually.

Tapestries of rich patterns used to hang against the walls. Carpets brought from exotic lands made with luxurious material were gone from the floors. Everywhere he looked he could see nothing but reminders of his father's waste and debauchery. The estate had once been a tribute to the family name, a fine and beautiful home, but now all of it was little more than a hair's breadth from utter ruin.

No, not a hair's breadth. A *wedding's* breadth. That was all it would take to save them, and everyone in MacMorton Castle knew it. He would marry Miss Horne and all the wealth that came with her. His castle would be saved.

Then he'd have to leave it. That was the deal. Miss Horne had made it very plain in her letters that she had no inclination at all to spend her life withering away in some God-forsaken castle in the God-forsaken midlands. She did, however, want a title. If he wanted her money—and by all accounts she had plenty of it, thanks to her generous father and his thriving merchant lines—Braden would have to marry her then spend his own life withering away in some God-forsaken city. London, to be precise.

But MacMorton Castle would be spared, and all his servants and tenants and the unlikely menagerie he kept would continue to eat. He simply would not be around to enjoy it. Still, he could hardly back down from his duty. And frankly, after finding Miss Horne in that mass of destroyed carriage last night, he was more inclined than ever to meet his responsibilities.

Even injured and waterlogged she was a beauty. He should be ashamed of himself for having noticed such a thing while the poor girl was barely clinging to life, but any mortal man might be excused under the circumstances. Especially considering that all reports of her appearance held her to be "handsome" or "passable." He'd been pleasantly surprised to find her so... well, pleasant.

To look at, at least. He'd not yet had the benefit of an actual meeting. Would she wake soon? Would she be appreciative of his efforts last night, braving that treacherous valley to find her then carting her all the way home? Would she feel lost and alone and turn to him for comfort, or would she view him as the reason her father was dead and she was alone? He would have to steel himself for either possibility.

Or perhaps she might demand immediately to be sent home, to call off their wedding altogether. She was an heiress, after all. With her father's passing she was now an extremely wealthy young woman. She may no longer wish to share that wealth with him.

He watched the servants bustle around, cleaning, polishing, and decorating the house with a fervor he hadn't seen since... since childhood. Perhaps they understood the situation just as he did. Of course he'd tried to keep it from them, to give the impression of success and security, but in a remote community such as theirs, with a staff of retainers who had been as family to him, he could hardly expect to keep many secrets. They knew Miss Horne represented far more than simply a bride for their master.

And apparently, they were putting forth extra effort to make her stay here as agreeable as possible. He loved them for it. He only hoped they would not find they were wasting their time.

"She is awake now, sir," Mrs. Garver said.

He turned, startled. He'd been so lost in thought he'd not heard his housekeeper's approach. She was gracious enough not to comment at his woolgathering.

"She's eaten a bit and I've given her the sad news of her father," she went on. "She took it well."

"It must all be very hard for her."

"Indeed, she seemed somewhat confused at first, but that's only to be expected. She asked many questions, but I think you will find her a very sensible, reasonable young lady."

"I'm pleased to hear it."

"And she cleaned up rather nicely, if I might say so, my lord."

He pretended to overlook her knowing smile. "I'm certain you mean her injuries are healing and she's

21

recovering quite well, Mrs. Garver."

The older woman laughed at him, as she always did. But he didn't mind. He'd lost his own mother in childhood and Father was off wasting their fortune most of the time, never bothering to find him a proper nurse. Mrs. Garver and the rest of the staff had filled the roles of nursemaid and parents for him. Braden would never forget that. The least he could do for them now was to follow through with his plan and marry Miss Horne. The sooner the better.

"I told her ye'd be up to see her, sir. She's eager to meet ye."

He hoped that was true. Indeed, he was quite eager to meet her. The next few minutes would likely determine the course of his life. Perhaps, then, eager was not quite the right word. Terrified might be more accurate.

Not that he'd ever let that show. One thing he did— and did well—was hide his emotions. That much his father had taught him. In spades.

The broth had been weak, but fresh and hot. That was surprising, considering the apparent size of MacMorton Castle. Back home at Wythelea Abby the kitchens were so far removed from any of the family areas that it was a rare treat to find dinner still warm. Cassandra couldn't help but feel she'd been given some sort of special treatment, receiving a hot meal expressly prepared for her at an odd time in the middle of the day.

And indeed it was the middle of the day. Apparently it had been nearly midnight before Lord Braden had found her in the wreckage and brought her here. She'd been quite incoherent for that whole ordeal, thanks to the beating her head had taken. A goose-egg sized protrusion there was still tender.

It had not stopped her from tending to her hair, however. Remarkably, she felt much revived after the light meal Mrs. Garver had brought up and was determined not to look a complete horror when time came to present herself to this Lord Braden. She supposed it was a good sign that after all she'd been through her vanity was still intact. She also supposed that didn't say much for Papa. This soon after a parent's unexpected demise most young ladies might be expected to focus on grieving and not caring whether their eyes had gone puffy. As this deceased was merely Edward Loring—a falsehearted reprobate—Cassandra felt no need to waste time with weeping and fainting. Her grief was best felt silently.

What she needed was to get on with the business of survival and puffy eyes would do little more than get in the way of that. Unless, of course, it seemed that some grand show of sorrow was expected by the people of this household. In that case she supposed she could come up with adequate tears. But first she needed to determine for certain that her host was no threat.

It seemed she'd have her opportunity. There was a knock on the door and Mrs. Garver let herself in. Cassandra had been ordered to remain in her bed, propped up with a huge pile of cushions and covered with blankets made soft by multiple washings. It was quite a comfortable place to be, as a matter of fact, and she rather hoped she might remain here just a bit longer. Just until her head might cease pounding and she could know for a fact that Mr. Rovish was gone.

"If you're up to it, miss," the aged housekeeper said with a somewhat overdone curtsey. "Lord Braden would like to speak with ye."

"Of course," Cassandra replied. "By all means, I'd love nothing better than to thank him."

The woman smiled, then pushed the door open all the way and stepped aside. A gentleman appeared there. Given the circumstance, Cassandra could only assume this was Lord Braden. He was not what she had pictured.

She wasn't quite sure exactly what she had pictured, but it was not this. To hear Mrs. Garver speak of her master Cassandra had fabricated a vision of someone much older, much larger, and not nearly so... beautiful. Indeed, this Lord Braden was almost too beautiful.

His features were perfect, unblemished as the carved marble sculpture of a god. He was not overly large, yet his presence filled the room completely the moment he entered. His wild hair was jet black, as were his eyes. They captivated her. It was not just the pure attraction of those huge, dark-fringed eyes glaring at her, searching her, but it was the expression in them. Sadness, concern. Concern for her? She could not help but hope it was so.

So intent was her hoping that she actually jumped when the man spoke.

"I'm glad to see you recovering, Miss Horne."

Drat, but she'd forgotten they still believed that was her name.

"Mrs. Garver and everyone has been very kind to me, sir," she said, struggling to break free from those eyes. "Thank you for finding me."

"It was Brutus, in fact."

"Brutus?"

"My hound. He heard the cries of your horse, is my guess, and knew something was amiss in the hills. I followed and he led me to you."

"Then I hope I will have opportunity to thank him, as well."

This seemed to thoroughly surprise the man. "You wish to see Brutus?"

"If he is not allowed indoors I suppose I can wait until I am better, of course."

"No, he is allowed, but I thought... that is..."

"Yes?"

"In your letters you said that you... well, I had the impression you do not much care for dogs, Miss Horne."

"Oh. Well, that was before I was rescued by one."

"I see. Then I will be most happy to arrange a meeting between you. I think Brutus would be very relieved to see you so well."

The man's conviction over his dog's emotional state made her chuckle. Grandmother had always scolded her for such things, making a pet of every creature she could find and claiming to commune with it. Now here was a grown man doing the very same. Whatever would Grandmother say? Pity the dear woman couldn't be here to see for herself.

"I will look forward to it," she said.

"As will I," her host replied.

He wasn't quite smiling, but she was certain she could detect a slight lessening of the gloomy shadow she'd seen in his eyes. Or perhaps it was simply her own concerns that were easing a bit. Surely any man who so valued the opinion of his hound could not possibly be in league with the likes of Papa or Mr. Rovish. Clearly he was a better judge of character than that.

Mrs. Garver took the opportunity to clear her throat and excuse herself from the room. Lord Braden gave her leave, but he remained. Things could perhaps get a bit awkward now, considering he and Miss Horne had obviously carried on some correspondence and Cassandra had no idea at all any things they may have discussed. Considering that he was a man and she was a miss, it might stand to reason that some of the correspondence had been of a rather personal nature.

Yes, this could get quite awkward, indeed.

"I must thank you again for rescuing me, sir," she said quickly, hoping to keep conversation on issues where she was already well-versed. "I do hope you will acknowledge your share in the endeavor. It was not Brutus alone who pulled me from the wreckage, I am sure."

"No, I'll admit to that. I only wish I had been successful in my attempt to save your poor father. Please, Miss Horne, accept my deepest sympathy for your sad loss."

"Thank you. It's hard to believe that he's gone. But I'm told he died swiftly, without suffering?"

"I saw every indication that was the case."

"So you examined the condition of our carriage? You could determine what caused the accident?"

Apparently he'd not recognized any evidence of the true cause of Papa's death, but if the man had noticed wayward gunfire damage, no doubt he'd have questions. Perhaps the local magistrate would be called in. He would ask questions and she'd be quite obligated to answer. Her identity would become known, as well as the scheme that she'd been dragged into. The kindnesses she'd found here would likely evaporate.

Worse, such a sordid story as hers would attract attention. People would talk and word would spread. Whoever had been waiting at whatever had been Papa's real destination might be nearby. They would possibly hear of her. Then they would come, and Lord Braden would have no reason to shelter her. He'd be only too happy to rid his home of a lying imposter.

She'd do well to see that none of that happened.

"It appears the roadway at the crest of the hill had been washed out by the recent rains," he explained. "The temperature dropped, causing it to be made slick with ice. Such a small carriage and only one horse, well... the driver lost control and you tumbled down into the valley."

"And you found the driver?"

"I'm sorry, yes. Had he been with your family long?"

"Er... not very. I just... it must have been very bad for him, sitting up on his perch that way with nothing to protect him."

"Yes, I'm afraid he did have a very bad way of it. His injuries were... severe."

So severe, it seemed, that no one had noticed the gunshot. That was in her favor.

"And you found nothing else?"

"Actually, I did wonder at something."

He'd found Mr. Rovish! Indeed, that was good news. She'd have to invent a quick story to explain another man's presence, and perhaps the discovery of a fired pistol, but that should be no difficulty. Why should Lord Braden not believe whatever tale she came up with? She could say the extra man was an uncle, or something. Papa's valet, perhaps, armed for their protection. Surely she was clever enough to come up with something plausible.

"I noticed something was missing," Lord Braden went on.

"Missing?"

"Indeed, and I thought it unusual."

"Er, what is it?"

"Baggage."

"What?"

"There was no baggage in your carriage. None spilled out on the ground around it, either. I thought that quite odd, to tell the truth. I've never yet met the lady who could travel for any time at all without quite an assortment of boxes and bags and whatnot."

"Oh, that. Well..."

Drat. She hadn't thought about that discrepancy. Papa had been very clear when he instructed her to bring nothing more than her daily reticule when she left the house that morning. It was to appear as if she'd been kidnapped from the street, taken by thugs while out shopping with her maid. If she'd packed a bag, of course everyone would have suspected things were not as Papa had wished them to appear.

Now of course the keen-eyed Lord Braden would know something was not right.

"I believe I understand," he said and she tried not to cringe noticeably. "You were not planning to stay, were you?"

"Er, what do you mean?"

"You came all the way out here, but you did not

plan to stay. Did you, Miss Horne? I suppose I expected as much."

"You did?"

"Yes. I knew you were not fond of the idea of traveling to such a remote place as this, especially not with winter coming on and Christmas just a few days away, yet I fear I was rather insistent."

"You were?"

He dropped into the chair beside her bed and let out a long, pained breath. The poor man's expression went even sadder than before and when he turned those huge, dark eyes on her again it quite nearly broke her heart.

"I had hoped your visit to my home would affect you, would put your mind in a more favorable bent. I am heartily sorry now that I insisted. Clearly you came simply out of a sense of obligation with no intent to stay, and now here you are, stranded and grieving for your father. Truly, you cannot know the depth of my sorrow at the pain this must be causing you."

"But you've been nothing but kindness, and your staff has made me so comfortable! Please, sir, you mustn't feel I hold you in any way responsible for what has happened to me."

"You are too generous, Miss Horne. I hope you... that is, surely it's unfair for me to bring up the subject now, but... I pray this has not turned you against the gracious acceptance you have given me. Please know that my sentiments have not changed. I still long fervently to make you my wife."

His wife? Gracious, was that the nature of their correspondence? Heavens, how awkward indeed! Her face went hot and she wished she could hide from the man.

He must be fully in love with Miss Horne even though never having met her. It was wrong, so very wrong for her not to correct his misunderstanding. Yet... what could she do? If he tossed her out now... no, she could not tell him. Then again, what if the real Miss Horne should appear? Indeed, *that* would be awkward beyond comprehension!

"Sir, I truly must tell you..."

Oh, but it was so very, very hard to go on. And with the man staring at her, hanging on her every word for some hope he might not be disappointed. Such a pity. Just where was the real Miss Horne, anyway? He seemed to doubt her commitment. What if the girl had already decided against her journey, as he'd indicated she seemed inclined to do. Perhaps the man's heart was already broken, he simply did not know it.

Then who was she to rush things along? And, after all, there was that little matter of her own life being very much in danger now. Perhaps God might forgive her just this once for continuing a falsehood. And who knew, perhaps Miss Horne might turn up after all— once Cassandra had arranged some safe escape for herself—and the man's heart would be spared. It might be considered a good deed to protect him now, mightn't it?

Lord Braden made it easy for her.

"I know what you will say. You cannot think of such things now. I understand. We will speak of it no more until you are stronger and can decide for yourself whether to stay, or to leave and head back home to London. There is no rush, I'm afraid. The road is quite gone and more clouds dim the horizon. I daresay you will have ample time to contemplate your future, my dear, before it is safe to consider departure."

She glanced over at the window. Indeed, she could see just enough to notice he was quite right. The gray haze had grown grayer, what clouds she could see were all foamy and full. It appeared to indicate snow, perhaps. Yes indeed, those roads were already impassible. The addition of more rain or inches of snow would completely result in her being quite trapped.

Hopefully, though, that meant whoever waited for Papa might also be trapped. They would have no means of learning her whereabouts. Perhaps this approaching bad weather was more her salvation than not. The real Miss Horne could not arrive, Mr. Rovish was gone, and Papa's cronies had no way to find her. She tried to contain her emotions. There might be time, after all, for her to make everything right!

"Thank you, sir," she said. "I can see not only are you a man of compassion, but honor and patience as well."

He smiled gently and nodded. Never had a man looked at her with such depth of feeling, such keen affection. Such love. She ached inside to know how little she deserved it.

Chapter 4

Lord Braden knew he was a horrible, despicable person. How could he treat that poor girl this way, act as if was some lovesick pup over her? He did not care one bit for Miss Horne. Her letters had been tedious and self-centered and left his heart cold and annoyed, not longing and desirous and any of the other sweet-sounding things he had hoped to convey. Anyone who would misrepresent himself in such a way as the woman languished there in her grief and her pain deserved nothing but rebuke.

Still, he'd fawned and batted his eyes and professed an imaginary *tendre*, all for the sake of his home. His home and his people and everything that he did love. He may be damning himself, but he'd be damned if he let them all suffer when something so simple as his marriage could prevent it. And luring Miss Horne was proving easier than expected.

The wreck had clearly shaken her. And of course the loss of her father left her broken and, well, vulnerable. He was a scoundrel to take advantage of that, but of course he would. It had been handed too neatly to him. A gift from above. Miss Horne was very literally at his mercy, and he would show her none.

He would be so gentle, so appealing, so gracious

and thoughtful that the girl would have no choice but to marry him. Quickly. And if she began to show hesitation, he would stoop to the most atrocious act possibly. He would make her fall in love with him.

He might even enjoy it. Oddly enough, he found this wounded but indomitable version of Miss Horne far more to his liking than the shallow, selfish creature he'd encountered through pen. He could credit it to her compromised situation and knew of course her true colors would undoubtedly shine through as soon as she was feeling more herself, but for now he could see the way clearly. She was reasonable. He would sway her. They all would.

In the end, he'd marry his heiress and rescue his estate. Then he'd have his full lifetime to be punished. For now, though, he'd make the best of it all.

He'd left Miss Horne with a gentle kiss on her hand and instruction to rest herself well. He'd sent Mrs. Garver with an overly generous portion of food for her meal. He'd taken their last presentable linens and sent them to her room for her use. He gave up what ration of coal he'd intended for his grate and sent it to her room for her comfort.

Miss Horne would never know just how desperate things were. She would enjoy her stay here at MacMorton Castle, he'd see to it. She would enjoy it so much she might decide not to leave.

And just for safe measure, he was in no hurry to send servants to make the road safe again. Best to keep things just as they were—Miss Horne lonely and feeling grateful with no easy way to leave. He'd kill her with kindness and then marry the girl on Christmas.

He had to. After that, there'd be nothing left here to

eat.

The light had turned grayer as the day had gone on. Cassandra snuggled deeper under the covers in the comfortable bed. The pain in her head was nearly imperceptible and her aching and bruising gave little reason to still claim such invalid status. She supposed she ought to get up, though it was tempting to simply remain.

Mrs. Garver had brought her a delightful late afternoon meal and the fire in the grate kept the room warm and snug. His lordship had not been back, so it was easy to loll about and forget the myriad troubles she knew awaited her attention. Staying in bed with a pile of books brought up from the man's library seemed a much better option.

She had slept more than she read, though, still exhausted from all that she'd been through. Still only half awake now, she shifted position to turn over and stare at the wall. Her pleasantly aimless gaze was disrupted by an object. No, two objects. Two eyes. She found them very near her face and staring directly at her. And they did not belong to Lord Braden.

Ordinarily that would have been a good thing, except that she quickly determined these eyes did not even belong to a human. Good heavens, but she had a large, bandit-faced badger curled up in bed with her!

She screamed. The badger jolted, sitting up on its haunches. It did not precisely scream, but made a high pitched growling, keckering sound. Who knew badgers could make such a noise? Cassandra struggled backward and promptly tumbled out of the bed.

Fortunately was not very painful, since she landed on something large and soft. Unfortunately, the large soft thing was a dog, who yelped and scrambled to its feet, trampling on her in the process. In terror, the poor animal leaped up onto the bed.

Which, understandably, sent the badger into further chuffing and wheezing. The dog responded by tumbling backward off the bed and onto Cassandra. She did not scream or chuff, but did wheeze a bit as the creature was heavy and managed to knock all the wind out of her.

At this point Mrs. Garver came screeching into the room and both animals dove under the bed, leaving Cassandra puffing and struggling to untangle herself from the voluminous night gown she'd been wearing quite comfortably just moments ago. She blinked up helplessly and found not one but two sets of eyes staring back at her.

This time, one set *did* belong to Lord Braden.

"I'm so very sorry!" he said quickly, appearing beside Mrs. Garver and stooping to help Cassandra up.

She was too much in shock to feel the full force of mortification at her situation. Her bare feet were cold on the floor, but at least they supported her as Lord Braden held her by the arm and steadied her. She glanced around, wondering if a herd of elephants might stampede through next.

None did, and she was somewhat relieved at that. Her traumatized head cleared and she was able to catch her breath again.

"What exactly happened?" she asked finally.

"You met Brutus, I'm afraid," he replied.

"I believe I landed on him. And he returned the

favor. But what on earth was that... that..."

"Badger," Mrs. Garver finished for her. "Sir, I told you the badger was *not* a good idea."

The badger seemed to agree. He was still growling from under the bed. Cassandra wondered if perhaps she should move a bit farther away from that item of furniture, but she wasn't entirely certain her startled, aching body could stand on its own without the aid provided by Lord Braden.

Besides, he smelled rather nicely of pinewood and spice. Odd, but it suddenly reminded her of home, all those long years ago before Mamma was gone and they would hang greens up to make the house festive for Christmas. Indeed, she'd very nearly forgotten the season was upon them again. How strange to remember it now.

"The badger has adjusted to living indoors," Lord Braden defended, then added almost inaudibly. "Nearly."

"The badger lives in the house?" Cassandra couldn't help but ask.

"Only until he is well enough to go back out with the others," Mrs. Garver said quickly.

"Indeed," Lord Braden agreed. "Provided this excitement hasn't aggravated his wounds, he should be healed up in no time."

Cassandra questioned this. "The badger is injured?"

He had appeared quite hale and hearty to her uneducated eye.

"He ran afoul of some roving dogs in a village not far from here. One of my tenants found him and knew that I... that is, I shall see that he doesn't bother you again."

"Oh, he did nothing wrong, really. I was simply a bit startled, is all. This is the first time I've woken to find a fat badger in my bed, you see."

The man very nearly smiled at that and she was entranced with the way such expression brought a light to his dark, brooding eyes and decorated his face with adorable little creases.

"And I assure you this is the first time he's climbed into a bed with someone so lovely as you," he replied.

Her face went warm. My goodness, was she blushing? Indeed, it seemed as though she was. The man was too kind, too near to her for comfort. She dropped her gaze and took two steps away.

"I'll see that he is removed to a more appropriate area," he said.

"No, please. Don't put the poor thing out on my account, sir. Now that I know he is here I'll be less surprised when I find him."

"Are you sure? You aren't afraid?"

She shook her head. "I'm not the one hiding under the bed huffing, you might notice."

"True. As a rule badgers are rather quite shy. I'm not even sure what brought this one out during the daylight."

"He was probably looking for a quiet place to sleep, and as I've been quite lazy today, this room must have seemed the warmest and coziest option."

"Thank you for being so gracious, Miss Horne. The last thing you needed was another great upset. I apologize for my wayward creatures and promise to work harder at containing them."

As he spoke, the huge head of a hairy-faced hound poked out from under the bed. He eyed Cassandra and when it appeared she was no threat, he began creeping out to lie at the feet of his master. Even lying down, the dog's head was very nearly at the top of Lord Braden's boot.

"This is their home, sir," she said. "I've no need to displace them. I'm sure Brutus and I will soon negotiate a peace, even if the badger might remain aloof."

"But you... are you certain? That is, I truly would not want to add further discomfort to your stay here."

"So far my stay here has been lovely," she said. "It was my journey here that left much to be desired."

He regarded her for a moment and she felt her face heating again. Her nerves had finally calmed just enough to begin feeling self-conscious, standing before him in a borrowed night gown and hair going every direction after a day spent lolling in bed. What must the man think of her!

Indeed, the upturn at his lips and the way his eyes searched her imploringly said he was very much thinking of her just now. She could in no way be comfortable with that! How could she? He thought she was someone else, someone he cared for.

"MacMorton Castle has never been graced with a more amiable visitor," he said. "I only hope you will never regret coming."

So far she quite rejoiced in her arrival here. Her only hope, in fact, was that *he* might not quickly regret her coming.

"You are tired," he said after an uncomfortable pause when she could think of nothing fitting to say. "Come, Brutus. We will let Miss Horne rest."

"But I..."

"Don't worry. We will have time to discuss things

tomorrow. You cannot think I would press you."

"No, of course not, but..."

"I'll send Mrs. Garver to check on you. If there is anything that you need, please ask."

He was starting to walk away, Brutus loyally at his side. She was glad for the fire in the grate, but her arms prickled with chill nonetheless.

"Thank you, but I... do you think..."

"Yes, Miss Horne?"

"Would you be able to get the badger out from under the bed please?"

He grimaced. "So sorry. I nearly forgot. It's just that I'm used to... that is, I'll take care of him."

He strode to the far side of the bed and crouched down. Holding his hand down to the floor he made some badger-ish clucking sound with his tongue and Cassandra held onto her breath. Would he actually coax the thing out from there?

It appeared that he would. The chuffing noise stopped and the gentle padding of four little feet sounded under the bed. Lord Braden pulled something out of his pocket, she noted. He waved it toward the bed, but did not hold it down close for the creature.

Amazingly, he did not have to. The badger appeared. She could see the tips of his ears as he crept out and climbed onto his lordship's makeshift lap. The badger's nose wiggled and his head bobbed up and down, following the scent of whatever was in the man's hand. At last he was secure in his master's firm grasp and the reward was allowed. It appeared that badgers didn't quite wag, but Cassandra was certain the animal's tail flicked up and down as he nibbled the little bits he'd been offered.

He seemed quite at ease with Lord Braden, not chuffing or growling as the man held him tight, rose to his feet, called for his dog, then bid Cassandra a good evening. She was quite amazed by it all.

"Sir," she called to him before he was quite gone. "Are there... er, will there be more of them?"

"More of what, Miss Horne?"

She dipped her head toward the badger in his arms. "Animals."

He let out a sigh. "Very probably, yes."

"I see."

"I will attempt not to loose them in the house," he assured her.

"Oh, I don't mind. I just... no kinds of snakes, are there?"

"No. Not at the present."

"Well then. I will try not to fall out of bed on anyone."

She smiled to let him know he need not worry she held a grudge toward his badger. He smiled back from the doorway.

"Rest well, Miss Horne."

"Thank you, sir. I will."

Of course she would not. How could she? She'd slept half the day. Besides, Papa was murdered, Mr. Rovish was still unaccounted for, the weather was bad, she had lied about her own name, and now she'd found a stray badger in her bed.

And on top of all that, Lord Braden's kind smile had done the most curious things to her insides! Indeed, it seemed resting would not be so easy. Not at all.

Lord Braden was still holding the badger when his groom came panting up to him in the corridor. He did not like the worry lines etched into the man's face, and the fact that he seemed barely able to catch his breath did not seem to bode well. His mind rummaged through all the things that could possibly be wrong.

"What is it, Drake? Has the carriage horse taken a turn for the worse?"

The groom shook his head. "No sir. He's doing well, no fever and he's holding weight on that back leg."

"Ah, good news. Perhaps it is not broken, after all. Has the bleeding been stopped to that gash in his shoulder?"

"Indeed, sir. The treatments you recommended have been just the thing."

"I'm relieved to hear it. So what, then, is your cause for such alarm now?"

Drake took a deep breath before continuing.

"It is Rovish, sir."

"Rovish? What's the old bastard done now?"

"He's got everything in place, sir. Guns, dogs... he'll be doing the deed."

"But the girl's here already, damn it. He'll get his full payment."

"Seems he wants to go about it his way and not yours."

"Damn it. I should have never trusted an agreement with that blackguard."

"So what's your plan, sir?"

Braden glanced up the length of the corridor. No one around, nothing but shadows to overhear them. Still, he feared even those. This was not a discussion he'd been eager for, and by God he would not let even a breath of it reach any other ears.

"Not here, Drake," he said. "And let no one hear word of this. Ever."

Chapter 5

Good gracious! What had she overheard? Cassandra
pressed her back against the door, panting and praying
that she'd heard wrong. Whatever was Lord Braden
talking about? Plans, agreements... with Mr. Rovish?
Lord Braden had been in on the scheme!

Cassandra had been so encouraged after his
kindness, but now what could she think of the man?
She was so grateful for all that he'd done, but perhaps
she'd been too hasty to give up her suspicions. Well,
thank heavens she'd not done as instructed and
remained tucked up in bed.

Instead, she'd fretted and worried that he'd been so
kind and so gracious, perhaps she'd not thanked him
enough. So, she'd left her bed and gone to the door,
knowing he'd still be in the corridor. She planned to
poke her head out and call to him, expressing gratitude
one last time for all that he'd done. When she peered
out, though, Lord Braden was not alone. She'd found
him greeting his man.

At first their conversation was soothing, talk of
Braden's concern for the horse, and she was ready to
shut the door and get back in her bed. But then she
heard that horrid, awful name. The man mentioned
Rovish. Indeed, Lord Braden seemed only too well

acquainted with the man. He spoke of deeds and payment and plans and agreement. And then he took his man off to discuss things in private!

This could mean nothing but the obvious: Lord Braden was in league with the enemy.

At least, that's how it appeared. But why did he call her Miss Horne? If he were with Rovish he would know who she was. He certainly hadn't acted as if he knew that. Perhaps he was not entirely in on the plot. It could be he knew Mr. Rovish was up to something, but did not know all the details. Indeed, that could certainly be. He hardly seemed the type to plot kidnappings. Still, why would he whisper in hushed tones and call his man into secret if he were not plotting something dishonorable?

It was hard to make sense of it. Lord Braden seemed so kind and so... Then again, she hardly knew the man. Simply because he was gentle with animals and free with his praise, she could not assume him above all reproach. Indeed, for all of his faults, Papa had never been cruel, yet he certainly did not end very well.

Lord Braden had an arrangement with Mr. Rovish so she mustn't dare assume herself safe. Pity, though. She'd rather found herself coming to like the dark-eyed young lord.

But looks could be deceiving. Perhaps she'd best start looking beyond his fine features and bottomless gaze. She ought to know just what she was dealing with here. To do that, though, she couldn't very well lounge here in bed any longer.

She crossed the room on unsteady legs and took hold of the bell pull. She wasn't the least bit hungry just now, but Mrs. Garver would not need to know that. A glance at the clock indicated the hour must be near dinner time. Perhaps she should not sit alone in her room and let Mrs. Garver bring another tray up to her.

Perhaps she was up for joining her host.

Lord Braden's office was dark and cold. The lone lamp he had glowing at his desk did little to illuminate beyond that single area and it did nothing to warm the air. He tried to convince himself Drake would not notice, but of course how could the man not? If it had been dropping snowflakes in the office there would be little difference indoors from the outdoors. Certainly the staff knew exactly how desperate things were, that Braden had taken to wandering his house in the dark rather than use up oil or burn through his thin supply of candles. And he'd taken to darning his own socks since he'd put his ancient valet on pension. He was darning them more frequently, too, as he'd taken to wearing multiple pairs to keep his feet warm.

But Miss Horne was here and most things would soon be better. Unfortunately, if Drake's worries were well founded it seemed time had run out for the issue with that damned, cruel Rovish.

"He's not willing to wait, not even another week?" he asked his groom behind the security of his office door.

"I'm sorry, sir. I got word he plans to host a party on Christmas Day. A hunting party."

"Damn. Those poor creatures haven't got a chance. He's raised them in ruddy boxes; they'll be lost when he puts them out to field."

"Doesn't seem the least bit sporting."

"As if Rovish cares about such a thing. And I'm so demmed close to having the price he wants to buy the animals from him!"

The groom shook his head sadly. "It just can't be fair. Are you certain there's no way you can get the money early from your little bride to be?"

Braden laughed at the mere thought of it. "After the woman was just mauled by my slobbering hound and nearly frightened to death by a semi-domesticated badger? No, I highly doubt she'd be in any frame of mind to fund my rescue effort for Rovish's captive fox population. Besides, with the lack of baggage that arrived with her, it's clear she had no intention of committing herself in any way. Whatever funds she has with her are clearly intended to pay for her journey home. Period."

"Well that certainly wouldn't be anywhere near what Rovish demanded to buy a reprieve for those poor animals."

"No, it would not be."

But obviously Drake knew his master too well. He lowered his voice and asked, "So what are we going to do?"

"I cannot include you."

"You haven't a choice, sir. Obviously something needs to be done, and I'm not letting you do it alone."

Braden shook his head, though. "It's too risky for you. I'm a peer, Drake. Rovish can't touch me. You, however, aren't quite as safe. If I can't scrape up the money to rescue a few unlucky foxes, I sure as hell won't be able to buy your way out if we get caught."

"Well, sir, we'll just have to see we don't get

ourselves caught."

"No, Drake, I just can't let you—"

"It's not a matter of letting me, sir. You're just going to have to stop me."

"You don't think I could do that?"

"I don't think you *would* do that. Now tell me, sir, what plan do you have? Two days left before the big day."

Braden scratched his head and paced. Brutus followed faithfully, his thick tail swinging back and forth. He seemed as content to trust his master as Drake was. Braden loved that his household—human as well as lesser creations—put so much trust in him, but sometimes the burden was a bit more than he could carry. They all needed him, relied on him, had faith in him. It would be such a shame when he let them all down.

"There's nothing we can do, Drake," he said, wishing he believed this might end the discussion.

"Of course we can, sir. We go get the little beasties and rescue them."

"Just like that?"

"Just like that."

"I'm fairly certain Rovish would see that as theft."

Drake seemed to care little for what Rovish thought of anything. He merely shrugged. "That's only if we get caught, sir."

"I've already told you what would happen if we get caught. I haven't a penny to cover a fine for either of us."

"You haven't a penny for much of anything, sir, yet here we are all well fed and sleeping under a dry roof. Somehow you manage that for us all. You'll manage to rescue them foxes."

Damn it, but the man was right. Braden did always find a way to accomplish what was needed, and those pitiful, underfed foxes being kept in Rovish's dirty boxes faced a very dismal future. They needed rescue. Of course he would do what he had to.

"Very well, Drake. May I suppose you've already determined where exactly we are going to put a dozen young foxes so that damn Mr. Rovish isn't likely to come find them?"

"Can't put them in the stables, sir. They'll set up to yelping and Rovish is bound to hear if he comes by."

"That's likely to be the trouble no matter where we put them."

"Unless you put them in the castle, sir."

"In the castle?"

"Walls built thick to fend off invaders, a maze of rooms like ruddy rabbit warrens, hiding holes leading God knows where... indeed, sir, if you put them foxes inside your castle, Rovish isn't likely to ever have a clue."

"In case you're not aware, Drake, I happen to have a young lady inside my castle right now. A young lady, I might add, who has declared to me on more than one occasion—in writing, no less—that she is not very fond of animals. She's already been more than gracious regarding that subject. I fear filling my home with desperate wild things might be more than she can stomach. I wish for her to marry me, Drake. Echoes of yelping foxes throughout the castle are not likely to further my cause."

"So we do nothing and Rovish takes his party out on the very day of our Lord's birth and blasts the little buggers into oblivion? Hell, even if any of them do avoid the hunters, they haven't got a chance living out in the wild. They been hand fed most of their lives, stuck in them damn boxes. They can't hunt, can't recognize danger, don't know the elements, won't last the month on their own."

"Oh, hellfire. Of course we'll go get them and bring them here. I'll hide them in the castle; there must be some forgotten corner in the bowels of this place where we can keep them until they are fit to introduce back to the wild."

"That's the spirit, sir! You've got a heart of gold, you do."

"If only I had a few less vital parts made of the stuff, Drake. I'd sell off an arm or a leg."

His groom seemed to think this was humorous. He laughed. Brutus wagged his tail and swiped a book off a nearby stool.

"That you'd do in a heartbeat if you could, sir. We all thank you for it, too. And those little foxes will be ever grateful, hopefully growing up to keep the rabbits from eating all your cabbages next year."

Hell, this year he ended up planting a row of the stuff outside the garden walls specifically for the local rabbits. He was a fool. Stealing away Rovish's live entertainment right under his nose was too great a risk. He was going to do it, of course, but he knew he'd regret it.

Trouble was, he'd regret it all the more if he did nothing and let Rovish's cruelty run free. The foxes had been caught on Braden's land, after all. If his dissipate father hadn't mortgaged it out and let it to Rovish, the wildlife would be safe from such treatment. Hunting

would be done humanely and of necessity, not sport.
Especially not Rovish's type of sport.

Once he had Miss Horne safely to the altar and
could claim her inheritance as his own, then he could
confront Rovish and pay back what was owed. He
could take back what Father had lost; what should now
be his. He could make it all well. The Braden estates
would be returned to their former glory and the name
would no longer be linked with dishonor and collapse.

Then he would leave it forever and live out the rest
of his life in some pestilent city. Damn, but he only
wished he could think his way out of that part of the
bargain. But a deal was a deal and if he had any hope
whatsoever of persuading Miss Horne, he needed to
assure her he would uphold his promise. Of course to
do that he'd have to make sure she wasn't run out of his
home by his creatures.

Not at all interested in cooperating with the plan,
the badger began squirming in his arms. He'd very
nearly forgotten the poor things. Indeed, it was getting
to be the animal's usual feeding time, no wonder he was
restless.

"Here, this is getting hungry and I think cook will
be expecting me for my dinner soon." He handed the
badger over to his steward. "Don't worry about the
Rovish situation. We'll take care of it."

Drake smiled and soothed the chuffing badger.
"When, sir? I'll have a couple lads on hand to help us."

"Tomorrow night." It was a spur of the moment
decision, but the groom seemed to concur. "We will act
tomorrow night, Drake."

"Sure enough. That damned old bastard, Rovish,
will never know it was us. He'll find no trace of us *or*

the dear little fox kits."

"I hope not. More importantly, I hope Miss Horne finds no trace of them."

Good God, if she found herself swarmed by a dozen frantic, malnourished foxes, she'd call for a carriage and drive herself back to London, with or without better roads. Somehow he'd just have to make sure she had no idea what he was up to. He'd have to act as if he had not a care in the world but to make himself the best bridegroom ever. He'd sweep her right off her feet.

Indeed, life was about to be very busy and very, very complicated for him. There was a distinct chance it would all end quite badly. There was an equal chance he'd end up with an attractive young wife he had nothing in common with.

Why on earth did he realize he was actually looking forward to all of it?

"Are you certain you feel up to it?" Mrs. Garver asked her.

Cassandra was not at all certain of any such thing, but she made a fair show at smiling confidently.

"Of course! You've been so accommodating, and I've slept nearly the whole day. I should very much like to move around a bit. Besides... I am awfully hungry and there's no reason at all for you to carry food all the way up here. If his lordship is eating downstairs, then I should simply go join him."

"If that is what you'd like, miss, but I assure you it's really no trouble to bring something up."

She put on a frown and wrung her hands together. "Would his lordship prefer that? I mean, I had not thought that perhaps he'd rather not see me. I must look a fright, after all, so who could hardly blame him for not wanting me at his table, and—"

"Oh, no miss! You're positively lovely! I'm sure that his lordship would be thrilled at your company. It is merely your health I'm concerned of, but of course if you say you are well..."

"Thank you, Mrs. Garver. I do appreciate your concern. It's so good to feel cared for."

The older woman took a break from working at Cassandra's hair and patted her shoulder.

"I understand, miss. You've been through a lot. It's no wonder you don't want another cold meal here alone."

"Thank you," she said. "I will try not to make his lordship regret it."

Mrs. Garver clucked her tongue and rattled on about how his lordship would no doubt enjoy her company over dinner. The housekeeper had nothing but glowing praise for the man and Cassandra could tell all of it was heartfelt. She suspicioned, though, that she detected just the tiniest bit of embellishment. Apparently Mrs. Garver approved the match between her master and the supposed Miss Horne and was eager to facilitate it.

But that was a good thing for Cassandra. She needed to be on good terms with the staff here. The more they grew fond of her, the less likely they were to allow her to be cast out into the cold once the truth all came out. Perhaps she could count on Mrs. Garver to give her a warm wrap or a parcel of food to take on her way. Indeed, she needed all the friends she could get at this time.

And even better, she had a chance to win over his

lordship. She touched up her hair and smiled at her pale reflection in the mirror. Not bad, considering she was still a mass of aches and bruises beneath the borrowed gown Mrs. Garver had found. By its outdated mode and threadbare material, she could only guess it had come from a rag bin. But it fit adequately well and with a shawl draped over her shoulders and her hair combed neatly in place, Cassandra had to admit she did not look completely dreadful, all things considered.

She hoped she would not be an embarrassment to Lord Braden's table. She hoped she would not be unwelcome there, either. The man had ordered her rest. He had not invited her to dinner. But how else was she to learn of his scheming with Rovish? How else was she to protect herself if she did not know the nature of danger she faced?

Dining with the man was unavoidable. It was for her own security, after all. She'd just have to make the best of it.

That, she discovered as she walked into the chilly but intimate room where Lord Braden was taking his meal, was not going to be as difficult as she imagined. Mrs. Garver led her to the room then cheerfully announced her to his lordship. He glanced up with surprise as she entered the room, but his face soon broke into earnest welcome when he saw her. She could not help but return his warm smile.

"Miss Horne! How delightful to see you appearing so well."

He rose and led her to the table, selecting a place directly at his right hand. The familiarity of it made her cheeks burn, but she kept herself calm. Perhaps a light blush would suit her and make the man more inclined to appreciate her presence.

"I'm so sorry to force myself on you this way, sir," she said, taking the seat he offered. "Mrs. Garver tried to convince me to rest, but I simply could not face another meal all alone."

"Of course," he said, stumbling slightly as he returned to his seat. "I should have realized how alone you must feel."

A servant appeared and bustled about to set a place for her. The service was neat, but Cassandra was surprised at the common nature of the plate set before her. Perhaps since she was not expected, his lordship's good tableware was not ready for use. It made little difference, though. She rather liked a more casual atmosphere. It helped soothe her nerves.

"I'm afraid I've never been a good invalid," she said brightly. "I can't abide being still very long."

"I suppose you've told me as much in your letters," he said, although the light faded just slightly in his huge, dark eyes. "You must keep very busy in London."

So that is where Miss Horne was from? Good. Cassandra knew London. She did not much care for it, to be honest, but convention dictated she'd been forced to spend time there upon occasion. Not exceedingly much, thank the good Lord, but enough to be familiar with most of the places a well-bred young lady would be expected to know.

"Indeed, I have friends and we go about to various places," she said and hoped he might not ask for details. "The opera, the museum, the park."

"And the shops, I've no doubt."

"Oh, yes, of course, the shops. Everyone must love to go shopping."

Everyone except Cassandra, it seemed. She found the endless dawdling over every little bauble and trinket to be tedious and tiresome. Now a bookstore, perhaps, that would be a fine place to spend a few hours and some of her pin money, but aside from that she'd far rather spend the time walking in one of the parks. Indeed, time spent indoors in London was the worst part of her days spent there. She was always happiest when Grandmother announced it was time to go back to the country.

"I only wish we had such pleasures to offer here," he said with a dreary shake of his head. "No doubt you will find yourself bored half to tears before long."

Oh, bother. She'd not meant to make the man unhappy with his own home! Indeed, she'd best redirect conversation if she did not hope to give him reason to resent her.

"Oh, but who can be bored wtih Christmas just two days away? It seems only yesterday it was Michealmas."

"Indeed. My servants have been enjoying the decorating, but..."

"But?"

"Well, I have halted that now, of course."

"Halted the decorating? But why?"

"Er... for respect of your father, of course."

"Oh. Of course."

She should have remembered the man expected her to be in mourning. And she was, of course, but not in the way that he thought. Papa's body may have only recently ceased function, but the man had been lost to her for years.

"The servants had wanted to put the castle to its

festive best for you, but of course now is hardly the time for celebration."

"Thank you, my lord. But... I hate to deprive the rest of the house. What festivities do you generally observe?"

He warmed to this question. "The decorating, of course. My lands boast proud forests and each year the whole house takes part in bringing in greens and selecting the yule log. And... well, in the past I have hosted a ball."

"A ball?"

"Nothing like what you must be accustomed to. No, merely a simple event with country dances and good company."

"So you are not as remote here as you seem. There must be a good number of gentry nearby."

"Er... something like that."

"Oh, but what fun. I do love Christmas in the country with all the local traditions, the warm sentiment, the gathering of friends."

"Really? Then I hope, even in mourning, Christmas at MacMorton might bring you that warm sentiment. I've instructed the servants to be mindful of your loss."

"Thank you but, please, allow them to enjoy the holiday, sir. I may have suffered a loss, but that is no reason for everyone to feel glum."

"That is kind of you, Miss Horne."

"It's the season for kindness, don't you agree?"

Indeed, and what better way to ingratiate herself with the staff than to assure their festive holiday? Perhaps if they did not resent her, they might help keep her safe.

Their dinner was served. She studied the food on

her plate and wondered if his lordship had some digestive troubles. What an odd assortment of garden vegetables in some type of weak gravy. The meat source for the gravy was altogether unidentifiable, primarily because there was none of it.

Apparently her confusion showed on her face.

"I hope you find your meal acceptable," he said. "I... er, instructed cook that I was not very hungry."

"It's fine, I'm sure," she replied, digging in with fabricated enthusiasm. Fortunately, it tasted far better than it looked. "My, but it is good. Truly, quite enjoyable."

"I will make sure to have something a bit more substantial for tomorrow's meal."

"Whatever you like, sir. Please do not think that you must strive to impress me."

"But Miss Horne, of course I will strive to impress you," he said, meeting her eyes with an intensity that very nearly caused her to drop her spoon. "I want my wife to be very impressed with me."

"How could she not be? Er, that is, I mean..."

"You are most kind, but I recognize it's hard to be impressed by a castle that's run over by badgers and ill-behaved hounds. I am determined to make amends."

"I think pulling me out of a smashed carriage and saving my life ought to count for some kind of amends."

"Do you? Well, then I am very glad that I did so. I hope that act helps make up for the disastrous encounter earlier."

"It was not so very bad. You worry too much. Indeed, the badger quite startled me, but I'm hardly the worse for it. Where did you put him, by the way? He's not been tossed out to the cold, I hope."

"I've put him in the care of my steward. I daresay Drake will keep him comfortable and fat. He is very good with the animals."

"So you were serious. There are other odd creatures besides that wayward badger."

"Did you believe I exaggerated in my letters?"

"No, but... er, yes, I suppose I did. Just what exactly sort of zoo do you keep here?"

"It's not my intent to run a menagerie, Miss Horne, I assure you. But my lands are quite teeming with creatures of all sorts and when we encounter one who has met with some injury, or been lost from its mother, or any manner of difficulty, I can hardly turn a blind eye, can I?"

"Of course not. Who could?"

"Some do, apparently. But you are correct; most people feel compassion. They bring them to me and I haven't a heart to turn them away. My stables, I fear, are more often than not filled with everything *but* horses these days."

What a dear man! No wonder Miss Horne had given consent and was planning to venture this far from the city. Indeed, what woman could possibly reject such a kind soul? And he came with a castle and title, as well! And those eyes. Yes, Miss Horne would be a very happy woman once she arrived to meet her intended.

If she arrived. For now, Cassandra had the benefit of enjoying his charm for herself. And those eyes.

"You are an angel," she proclaimed him. "But I must thank you for not relegating me to the stables with all your other rescued creatures."

"I hope you are finding the castle infinitely more

comfortable than a stable, my dear. Have you been warm enough?"

"Quite so. Your servants have kept the fire going nicely and my room is very snug."

"I'm glad to hear it. I worried you might find the place too drafty for your constitution."

"No, but I'm finding myself dreadfully curious. From what I've seen, the castle must be remarkably old. Has it been in your family all this time?"

It was clear she'd selected a subject quite near to the man's passion. She was spared having to say much as he went on telling stories of ancestors who fought this battle or that, served one king after another, and who seemed to each build some wing onto the castle. He confessed much of it had fallen into disrepair, but obviously that did nothing to diminish his love of the place, or his pride in it. No wonder he was eager to bring in a wife and fill the place with giggling heirs and all the warm, familial sentiment Cassandra was always jealous of when she detected it in other families.

"I could show it to you," he said when he finally paused to glance up and realize she was still listening to him. "That is, if you are up to it tomorrow."

"Of course," she said with honest enthusiasm. "I'd like that very much."

He nodded, a fresh sparkle in his eye giving way to his own honest enthusiasm. "Very well. Tomorrow you get a grand tour of MacMorton Castle."

"I will be looking forward to it, sir."

"But you must promise to get a good sleep tonight."

"The castle is so huge that I need to rest up before seeing it?"

"No, but I wish for you to be well-rested before

facing the place. It is, I fear, not quite up to its former glory."

"I see. Yes, I've heard it can be quite a challenge to keep up with these old bastions."

Indeed she had heard. Grandmother complained constantly about the aging state of Wythelea Abby, though of course things were never as dreary as Grandmother declared. But she'd visited her great-uncle a time or two, and he had recently pulled down the old family manse in favor of building a very grand new home. It had seemed quite a pity to her, but even Grandmother claimed she was not sad to see the old place gone. MacMorton Castle, however, seemed safe from such fate, if Lord Braden's fondness and pride for it were any fair gauge.

"I suppose you see little use for maintaining such a relic," he said absently, going back to his food.

Cassandra thought before answering. "Is that what I said in my letters?"

"I determined as much, though of course you're too polite to speak disparagingly about my family home."

"Well, if that is what I inferred, I certainly cannot agree now. My impression of your home is quite favorable, and I'm certain my tour of it tomorrow will only strengthen that sense."

She'd obviously given the right answer. He smiled like a happy child.

"I hope so, Miss Horne. I do hope so."

Heavens, but her face was nearly on fire. She had to drag her eyes from his smile and concentrate on her plate. The real Miss Horne was a lucky, lucky woman. Even if Lord Braden did have some dealings with Mr. Rovish, Cassandra could in no way see him as any sort of a villain. He seemed everything kind and caring and honest. He deserved so much better than her self-serving lies.

Chapter 6

How long had it been since he'd enjoyed his evening meal? Ages. Usually the hours from sundown until he was ready to retire for the night seemed to drag painfully slow. As much as he loved his life here in the castle, there were times when the solitude grew heavy on him.

Tonight, however, his spirits were decidedly light. Miss Horne had proved charming and inquisitive and pleasant. Nothing like the woman he'd come to know through her letters. Could this really be the same person? It hardly seemed possible.

Except that he knew that it was. Ridiculous to even consider any other possibility. After all, there was hardly a surplus of attractive young ladies wandering the hillsides. Who else could she be? There was a perfectly logical reason Miss Horne was not acting like herself.

Trauma. Indeed, she'd suffered injury and the terrible pain of losing her father. Of course such dramatic events would be enough to put anyone off balance. For a pampered young miss used to comfort and privilege, no doubt she was in shock. He could hardly expect her to act like herself.

Therefore he would do well not to put too much

stock into her kind words and agreeable nature. It would only end badly if he began to have hope now. No, there was not hope and he'd already come to terms with that truth. He would marry her, yes, but he could not let him hope for anything more than that. No matter how much he might wish it.

But what if this distressing ordeal was more than a mere experience to be endured then forgotten? What if everything she'd been through had a profound and lasting impact? Wasn't there the slightest chance that she might truly be becoming the woman he was getting to know now? If so, then he might have every reason to hope. She might come to love his home, might be willing to stay. Hell, she'd even been friendly toward Brutus. How could he not let himself start developing hope?

No, he was probably being a fool. A person didn't simply become someone else over night. Perhaps for a time this great upset would alter her character, but surely in time she'd revert to her more normal state. Her wounds would heal, her grief would subside, and she would long for the life she once loved so much. But for a time, at least, he could…

But that was unfair. Wanting her to become someone else was to wish ill on her. After all, she needed to recover from trauma, not live in an altered state. And indeed, this Miss Horne was drastically altered from the original.

What if this change signaled something serious? A brain fever, perhaps. Or unseen injuries internally. It had been a most destructive accident. The sight of that coachman… well, the man had been a twisted, bloody wreck, with wounds Braden had not been able to comprehend. So much blood! Miss Horne was lucky to have been unconscious. If she'd crawled from that wreckage and seen for herself, well, she'd be damaged indeed.

If he was any sort of gentleman he'd stop rejoicing in the fact that she was proving much more agreeable to his plans than expected and he'd start worrying there was something terribly wrong with her. The girl needed medical attention. He should have sent men out to find a safe route so a proper physician could be brought in, not let himself sit over dinner and admire her eyes and enjoy her delightful conversation.

Yes, he should do it and he would do it. He'd put his own wishes aside and look after her. In fact, that might even work in his favor. If the physician proclaimed her ill, he would insist they marry straight away so there could be no hint of scandal as she remained here until she was well. If she was deemed well, then he could feel little guilt at taking advantage of her sudden amicability. Either way, her interests would be cared for as well as his own. His conscience could be clear and he'd still meet his responsibilities where his household was concerned.

At least, his conscience was clear as regarding Miss Horne. There was still that little matter of Rovish and his unfortunate little foxes. His conscience was not so very clear on that count.

He checked the clock on the mantle. It was late. Dinner was long over, Miss Horne sent up to bed, and most of the house was asleep. Drake should be here any moment to make their plans for tomorrow. When they would commit robbery and pray not to be caught.

Not that he feared for himself. He'd find some way

to talk himself out of any real repercussions. Likely he'd even find way to keep Drake and their men safe from reprisal. But Miss Horne... what would she think of his actions? He couldn't quite convince himself he didn't care what she thought. One truth he had told her at dinner.

He did want his wife to be horribly impressed with him.

She shouldn't have let herself doze on and off most of the day. Here is was dark and very, very late at night and she was wide awake. Usually her days were fairly active with walks and visits to neighbors and trips to the shops in the little town near the abbey. She kept herself well occupied with a wide range of interests and charitable efforts so that by the time she climbed into her bed, sleep drifted over her easily. Not so this night.

Perhaps it had been her lack of exercise, but more likely it was everything else. How was she to make her brain settle down for the night? She hated to call on a servant, although something hot to drink would have been nice. Reading would have been good, as well, except her candle had gone out and she'd rummaged as best she could in the dark but found no others in any of the drawers or cupboards in her cozy bedroom.

She tried opening the grate to borrow light from the coal fire inside, but the room began to fill with smoke and that was no good. It seemed forever that she'd been lying there, staring into the darkness and jolting at every strange sound in this stranger's home. She simply could not fall asleep.

And it was just as well that she was not asleep. If

she had been, she would have missed the soft scritching sound at her door. Her ears perked, and at first she thought she'd imagined it, but then it sounded again. Something most definitely was at her door.

After the Brutus and badger episode earlier she was a bit hesitant, but when the scritching sound was accompanied by a pitiful mew, she couldn't help but leap out of bed. Her strained muscles argued, but she hurried to the door and pulled it open.

Sure enough, there was a kitten. It was a tiny thing, all fluffed ginger fur and huge round eyes. It blinked up at her and mewed again. Oh, but this was infinitely better than a badger. She scooped the tiny thing up and snuggled it.

"What on earth are you doing here?"

It kneaded its paws against her skin and purred. She rubbed it behind its tiny ears. Where did it come from? It was clearly too young to be wandering this huge castle alone. It must have a mother somewhere. But where?

She scanned up and down the dark corridor. No sign of anyone, just cold, lonely darkness. Well, blue-tinted moonlight streamed in at the far end of the corridor, so it was not completely dark. And what was that sound? She was almost certain she heard something.

Yes, another quiet mew. There must be another kitten, which probably meant there was a mother cat somewhere nearby. She'd have to go find it.

The house was so still she didn't worry about being seen. She'd simply tiptoe to the end of the corridor, find whatever was making the mewing sounds there, and deposit this kitten with it. Or, perhaps she'd grab up that one as well and bring them both back to her room. It would rather be nice to have a little company.

Double checking for anyone in the vicinity, she was reassured of her solitude. Hugging the kitten to her chest, she darted out, pulling the door shut behind her and scurrying as silent as a mouse in her bare feet. The purring kitten made more sound than she did. It was so warm and so soft in her arms, she was already coming to regret the thought of leaving it, even with a mother and siblings.

But when she reached the far end of the corridor, all she found was an ill fitted window pane and wind whispering through it that sounded remarkably like mewing. There was no sign of another cat, large or small. How perplexing. Just where did this little muff come from?

She was about to carry it back to the warmth and security of her room when footsteps alerted her. She ducked back into the shadows of the nearest access corridor. Best to stay out of view until she knew who else was prowling this late at night!

Peeking around the corner, she soon had her answer. Lord Braden came into view. How odd to find him here. She watched and was a bit surprised when he stopped before her bedroom door. Very unexpected! What could the man hope to find visiting her in the middle of the night?

He raised his hand as if to knock, but then another set of footsteps sounded beyond him. She slunk deeper into the shadows, but kept one eye on the corridor. The kitten purred against her and she half feared it was loud enough to give her away. Apparently not, though. Another man appeared and approached Lord Braden. The same man she'd seen with him earlier.

"Have you got her yet, sir?" the man asked.

Cassandra held her breath.

"Not yet," Lord Braden replied quietly. "I was assuming she must be in here."

He indicated her room and she was pleased the man had assumed wrong.

"Awkward, sir. Getting caught would mean trouble," the second man cautioned.

"It's late. Miss Horne is probably fast asleep."

Making her completely vulnerable to whatever "trouble" he had planned. Well, how dare Lord Braden show up at her door in the middle of the night and suppose that... well, how dare he suppose *anything* about her in the middle of the night! And to discuss it with his man!

To think she'd believed him harmless, an honorable gentleman! What on earth could he have been planning to do?

Perhaps she did not want to know. After all, he did believe they were engaged to be married. It was entirely possible the man had planned to... well, thank heavens this kitten woke her before anything shocking could happen.

"I'm sure you'll be very discreet, sir," Braden's companion said, clearly not at all off-put by such dastardly goings-on. "I thought you should know we've got everything ready."

"That was quick."

"I put sturdy lads on it, sir. Didn't tell them what we're planning to do, though."

"Good. The less everyone knows about this, the better."

"That's my thinking, too. They didn't ask questions,

just set to work setting up a cell for our soon-to-arrive company."

Cassandra frowned, not missing the conspiratorial tone in this older man's voice. What on earth was Lord Braden up to? A *cell*? As if for a prisoner? She listened carefully, but her sense of alarm merely grew heightened as their conversation went on.

"Seems somewhat unneighborly to deposit our 'company' down in the dungeons, Mr. Drake," Braden said lightly.

Mr. Drake merely laughed at such a suggestion. "Unless you want this company taking off and running amuck, you chose the best spot, if I might say so, sir. We'll make it safe and secure down there. Once they're down, nobody's getting out."

"Or in, I hope. That's all we need, someone poking around and finding us out."

"Not going to happen, sir. The place locks tight and is soundproof. No matter of howling or crying can be heard beyond that level."

"I guess that's the nature of a dungeon," Lord Braden said with a shrug. "If all goes well, the incarceration shouldn't be needed too very long. Training shouldn't take too long, and as for consequences... well, I am hopeful a wedding is in my very near future."

"Delighted to hear it, sir. I never doubted your ability to charm."

"Well, let us hope once plans are put in action tomorrow night I've not lost that ability. I have a feeling our dealings with Rovish will require all the charm I can muster."

"Good luck with that, sir. I fear your charms are

best played out upon young ladies... and kittens."

Lord Braden chuckled at that, but Cassandra drew in a sharp breath. The words echoed inside her head.

He had plans for tomorrow night and dealings with Rovish? She tried and tried to make sense of that in any way possible that would not leave Lord Braden seeming a monster. She could not. Her host had deceived her! He was not a kind, compassionate saint. He was in league with a murderer and had plans to lock her in a dark dungeon until she agreed to marry him! *Training*, he'd said. Is that what he thought his intimidation would be?

She had to escape. But where could she go? She had no feel for this place, had nothing but a thin nightgown and a kitten. How was she to save herself with only that? She ducked back into the corridor, staring into the dark, praying for some flash of inspiration.

"Let us hope that charm doesn't fail me now," Lord Braden was saying. "Miss Horne will hardly be pleased to find yet some other unwanted guest in her bed."

Indeed, he was right about that! Her heart pounded in her chest. It was late at night and yet the man had come here, to her very door, with despicable things on his mind. No doubt he'd be displeased to find her gone. What would he do?

What could *she* do? She squinted into the shadows. Her eyes slowly adjusted and she could detect the dark outlines of doorways. This small access passage was lined with doors. No, one doorway did not have a door. It was merely a dark, gaping maw that seemed to lead only into more darkness. She crept nearer to it. Ah, but it was a staircase!

Thank heavens, she'd found her escape. This was a

servant's staircase that would take her down, away from this area. She could find someplace to hide, perhaps clothing to wear. When daylight arrived, she could...

Wait, was that light? It was. The empty hole of the staircase was slowly illuminating with a flickering warm glow. Someone was coming up, carrying a light!

She peeked back out into the main corridor. Lord Braden and his man were still there. Oh please, why did they not leave? She was about to be caught!

The kitten wheezed as she clutched it so tight. She nuzzled it and breathed an apology. Poor thing. He simply kneaded away and purred all the more.

She watched as, ever so slowly, Lord Braden opened her bedroom door. Yes, go inside. Perhaps that would leave this main corridor empty just long enough for her to creep by, to find some other dark niche or some unused room to hide. And they'd best hurry, too. That glow in the staircase was now spilling out into the small passage where she hid herself.

But Lord Braden did not barge into her room. He timidly pushed open the door, then let his companion hold up a light. Drat. It only took a moment for her absence to be detected.

"Miss Horne?" Braden whispered. Then raised his voice louder. "Miss Horne?"

He pushed wide the door and at last went inside. In a heartbeat he came back into view. Cassandra was jumpy with nerves.

"She's not here, Drake!" the earl practically shouted. "She's gone!"

"Gone, sir? Where could she go?"

"The devil I know! Delirious, perhaps; gone off balance. We've got to find her!"

"Of course sir, we will."

Not if she could help it, they wouldn't. She turned on her heel to run but found herself face to face with a burning taper. Being held by a boy. Light filled up the passage and there was no way to deny it. She'd been found.

The boy blinked at her and she blinked at him. His eyes trailed up and down over her then he broke into a smile.

"Here she is, sir! I found her!"

Chapter 7

For a moment Braden wasn't certain he could trust his eyes. Indeed, though, Miss Horne was safe. She stood at the far end of the corridor, wide eyed and shivering in her thin gown. Was that a kitten she clutched as if for dear life?

Yes, it was. The very kitten he'd come up here in search of. Damn. But it had indeed done just as he'd feared; it had made a nuisance of itself and awoken her. He'd hoped to find it before that occurred. He could only hope this additional annoyance might not undo all the goodwill their pleasant dinner had built up between them.

From the expression on her face, it appeared that it had. Perhaps she was not a cat person.

"What on earth is all this, my lord?" she asked angrily.

"Forgive us, Miss Horne," he said. "I'm so sorry for the disturbance tonight."

"Are you? Then perhaps you might not have come here."

"Er, we were looking for that kitten. It was misplaced by its mother."

From the expression on her face he could see she found this hard to believe. Indeed, it must have seemed unlikely that, once again, he'd been so careless with his pets. She was clearly not only upset at the disruption of her sleep but she doubted his ability to keep his word. From the angry gleam in her eye he wondered if she might also be a bit suspicious of his intentions.

Not that he could truly blame her. So far her visit here had been anything but pleasant for her and he'd been able to do little to make it better. He—and his animals—had been making it consistently worse.

"Please, Miss Horne," he said, trying not to fumble his words. "I'm so very, very sorry. If you'll just hand over the kitten, I'll—"

But she seemed resistant even to that suggestion. She held the tiny bundle of fur more tightly and glared at him.

"The kitten is just fine, sir, and I will be, too, as soon as you and your entourage leave me to get back to my bed. Alone."

"Well, yes... of course," he said. "I just... that is, the kitten needs..."

"Oh, very well. If you promise to take her back to her mother and see that they are all very well, I suppose it would be best."

"Indeed, yes, it would. I can assure you the kitten would be fine. Are you... do you rather like kittens, Miss Horne?"

"Of course I like kittens. What sort of a person wouldn't like kittens? I was surprised to find this one wandering alone, so young as it is. I'm glad to hear it has a mother close by and that you claim to intend to reunite them."

"Certainly I'll reunite them. That's what I was hoping to do, why I came up here."

"And you needed two others to help you? What sort of kitten did you think you were tracking, my lord?"

"I was tracking that kitten and nothing else, I assure you, Miss Horne. I am deeply sorry it woke you and I can promise no one else will disturb you."

She was clearly unconvinced. Of course what reason did she have to trust him? And with her recent trauma, he could certainly understand the woman's misgivings. He would clearly have to see to better care for her. For everyone's well-being.

Especially since she did quite honestly seem to be concerned about the welfare of this nameless and wayward kitten.

"Very well. If you assure me the kitten will be well, I will let you take it," she said as if she were relinquishing the crown jewels. "But I should very much like to see it again tomorrow, if that might be arranged."

"Indeed it might. I could have the entire cat family removed to your chambers if you want for company."

She actually seemed surprised at the suggestion. Surprised in a good way, for a change. "You might? I believe I would rather like that, sir."

"Consider it done, Miss Horne. Now, please forgive all this interruption and return to your rest. All will be well. I promise."

"I hope so, my lord."

She regarded him, then eyed the distance between their little group and her bedroom door. He stepped to the side, clearing her path. No doubt she was feeling self-conscious, standing here in the corridor with them, wearing nothing more than the thin gown his servants had provided her. He himself was feeling a bit self-conscious, as well, though likely for different reasons. He shifted his gaze from her and cleared his throat loudly when he realized Drake was still staring. The man had the good sense to suddenly become interested in the ceiling.

"Sleep well, Miss Horne," Braden said.

She glared at him, then at Drake and then at the boy. Reluctantly handing the kitten over, she nodded then hurried past them into her room. She spared one last glance in his direction before she slammed the door shut. He heard the lock turn.

The kitten writhed, scratching him slightly. It merely made him smile. Yes, he supposed he'd be unhappy too if he'd been forced to give up a cozy position, snuggled against Miss Horne's warm breast.

They were silent a moment, then the boy spoke.

"That *is* the kitten you were after, ain't it, m'lord?"

"I believe it is, Peter," he replied, his mind not at all lingering on the kitten. "I do believe it is."

Drake took the boy by the shoulder. "Well then, back to the stables with us, lad. We've got a fair parcel of work in the morning. My lord, you'll take care of that little thing?"

Braden nodded. "I will, thank you, Drake. I'll take care of everything."

What could he mean by that? She leaned against the door and pressed her ear against it. Nothing more was said. The men's footsteps echoed at first, then got fainter until they disappeared completely. They were gone.

How dare the man show up at her door in the

middle of the night? If she had not already determined to get away from this place as soon as possible, she would have decided it now. Something highly irregular was going on and Papa had already been killed over it!

So Lord Braden was prepared to hold her captive in his dungeon until she married him. She did not care for dungeons and she certainly was not about to let Lord Braden coerce her into marriage. Even if he did believe her to be someone she wasn't, she was not planning to remain here long enough for him to learn the truth. Once she did get away—and she would—she must find the real Miss Horne and warn her.

But of course she'd first have to get away. Her first foray out of her room had ended in discovery, and this was the middle of the night. How on earth was she to creep out unseen in broad daylight? She had the gown Mrs. Garver gave her to wear to dinner, but where was her coat? Surely it would raise suspicion if she asked for it.

Plus, even if she did procure warm enough clothing to go out of doors, she could hardly expect to walk all the way back to civilization. She would need transport, and money.

Ah, but she knew where to find the latter. Papa. Well, with his body, at least. He'd whispered to her early on that he'd hidden a goodly sum in his clothing. It was sewn in, according to him, and not even Mr. Rovish knew about it. Papa had been rather proud of his forethought, actually. She'd been surprised not that he'd thought to hide the money, but that he'd had any of it in the first place. But he'd claimed that he did and she could only hope he'd been honest. For once.

She needed to get to his body. Indeed, that would

not seem so strange. He was her father, after all. It would be only natural that a grieving young lady would wish to see the body of her dearly departed Papa. Yes, and she'd ask for a moment alone. Surely no one would think anything amiss in a request such as that.

That left only the problems of finding a way out of the castle unseen then securing a carriage. Rather daunting problems, indeed! How could she surmount them?

Well, his lordship had promised to give her a tour of his castle, hadn't he? He did seem remarkably devoted to the place. She would simply remind him of his promise and he'd be quite happy to show her around. She would use that as her opportunity to plot an escape. Yes, surely in such an old, mazelike place such as this it would be impossible for servants to be in every corner at every moment. She would keep her eyes open to find the least populated areas and memorize every room, every corridor. Then she would escape.

Perhaps she could use Papa's money to bribe one of the servant's into procuring the transport for her. Yes, that seemed a plausible consideration. Of course that would rely on her finding enough money in Papa's secret stash to lure someone into such transgression, and then she'd have to find someone disloyal enough to accept her bribe. But she could do it. She'd have to do it.

And she had just one day. Lord Braden had indicated whatever he had planned would be set into motion tomorrow night. By that time Mr. Rovish would know where she was and would be involved. If Lord Braden's plans weren't devilish enough, she had no doubt Mr. Rovish's would be. And his lordship had seemed only too confident that things would end up just the way that he wanted them.

"I'll take care of everything," he had said.

She would simply have to see that he did not. Perhaps, just perhaps, the man could be somehow distracted from his scheme. Did she have the means to distract him? She had no choice but to try.

Chapter 8

Braden glanced up from his breakfast. Miss Horne came gliding into the room. Thank God, she was joining him this morning. He half expected her to be still furious and avoiding him. He was slightly embarrassed to admit how happy he felt that she was not.

And that she looked so well. At dinner last night she had seemed pale, and he'd been concerned that she should not have been moving about so much after her ordeal. Then there was the trouble over the kitten in the night. He worried it had all been too much.

Apparently, it wasn't. Miss Horne was radiant. He could only imagine what the woman might look like if she'd not just lost her father and been through a nightmare. Actually, he'd do well *not* to imagine her any more turned out than she was. He needed to keep his mind on all the many matters at hand. An even fresher and more lovely Miss Horne would have done serious damage to his concentration.

He'd already caught himself gaping wide eyed with a forgotten sausage on his fork.

"Good morning, your lordship," she said.

He thought for a moment he heard birdsong.

"Er, good morning, Miss Horne. Did you eventually

sleep well?"

"I did indeed. I'm so very sorry I was somewhat short with you last night. I do hope you can forgive me."

"Yes, of course. I'm to be faulted for disrupting your rest."

"Don't be silly. It was the kitten who disrupted me. I do hope she and her little family are well today?"

"They are. I saw to the mother's breakfast myself and took a careful inventory of kittens. All five are accounted for."

"Oh, but I do hope I get to see them. Five kittens! What could be more precious?"

What indeed? Except perhaps sharing his breakfast table with Miss Horne. He cleared his throat and dropped the sausage, finally regaining himself enough to remember to help the lady into her seat before returning to his. He thought he caught sight of one of his servants snicker at him.

"I shall see that you and the entire cat family make one another's acquaintances today."

"Excellent," she said and smiled directly at him. "And I do hope you recalled last night that you promised to show me around the castle. I am truly looking forward to learning all its secrets, and meeting the servants, of course."

"Certainly, if you feel you are up for so much activity."

"Heavens, do I still look such a fright?"

"No! I did not mean to imply that at all. Indeed, you look... er, that is..."

She sighed and shook her head. Her chestnut curls brushed against her ivory skin and she tipped her huge blue eyes toward him. By God, did she need to put her plump little lip out like that and pout? The woman made it dashed difficult to focus on eating.

"I'm sure I look like a woman who's just been in a terrible carriage wreck and has lost her dear father. I'm so sorry I can't make myself something smarter for you to have to look at today."

"If you were any smarter, Miss Horne, I'd... well, you need not fear for your appearance. I do not flatter when I say MacMorton Castle has never been graced with your equal."

"Why Lord Braden, you flatter me! Please, enough of this. I appreciate your kindness, but I'm afraid I do have a more somber matter to bring up."

"By all means."

She paused, a shadow coming over her lovely face as she absently pushed food around on her plate.

"I want to... that is, I've been thinking of... my father."

"Of course. I was waiting until you were recovered to bring up the subject."

"Thank you, but I'm sure this is not something that can be put off. Where is... I mean, what have you done with the body?"

He tried to be as gentle as possible with his reply. "The ice house."

She nodded, dropping her head and very possibly fighting back tears. He wished to God he was on close enough terms with her to give her the comfort she clearly needed, but of course what comfort could a near stranger provide? Then again, they'd corresponded for months, agreed on terms, in fact. How could he still consider them strangers?

Because they were. Every day the woman surprised him, proved how little he truly knew her. He had no right to think of himself as anything more than a recent acquaintance. What could he possibly do to help ease the pain she must feel over losing her father?

But then again, he intended to marry her. Perhaps he was not her closest friend now, but once they were wed he hoped to make her a jolly sight closer. What the devil could it hurt to try and start the process now? He slid out of his seat and moved to kneel beside her. She jumped a bit when he placed his hand over hers where she clenched them in her lap. He jumped a bit, too.

"I'm so sorry, Miss Horne. I cannot imagine the grief you must feel."

She blinked rapidly and tried to maintain a smile. "Surely you must know some of it, sir. You would not have your title if you had not lost your father."

"Yes, I have lost my father, but I'm ashamed to say he and I were never... well, he was rarely with us here and had little use for me, I'm afraid. Other interests occupied his time."

She was quiet, the smile fading completely. He felt altogether a cad for mentioning his own sad story when he had truly intended to provide comfort for hers. Clearly she and her father shared a much closer relationship than he had ever known with his. He should never presume to equate any part of his loss with hers.

"I think perhaps losing someone when there is so much distance between you is even harder than losing someone quite dear," she said softly. "You've lost not only that person, but any hope you ever had of the relationship that should have been."

"Insightful, Miss Horne, but I pray you not dwell on it. I've long settled with my past. You are what matters now, and you have suffered enough."

She went silent again, but did not pull her hands from him. He rubbed them slightly, comfortingly. He would do his best to help her through this, even if he hadn't the slightest clue how to truly grieve for a father.

"I'd like to go see him," she said finally.

"See him?"

"Yes, if I may."

"Er, we've had him and your driver in the ice house since we brought them here, but that's been two days. Are you very certain you should see him?"

"Yes. I am. May I, please? I think it will help."

"Well, if you truly think it will help you, I suppose I can take you there."

It was truly the last thing he wanted to do with her, but for her sake he'd do it. He supposed in some measure he could understand her need to see the body, have one last contact with her father as she decided what steps to take next. He'd tried to ignore it, but the fact was they could hardly plan a wedding when two bodies awaited burial in the ice house.

If she was up to it, the best thing to do would be to attend to that matter quickly so he could proceed with his plan. Despite how much he wanted to give her time, the fact was he simply did not have it. He needed a wife and he needed one for Christmas.

"Thank you, my lord," she said, smiling at him with dewy eyes and squeezing his hand affectionately. "Can we go now? I find I'm not very hungry."

By Hades, with her skin on his and her trusting expression, he would likely have done anything she asked. He only hoped she didn't ask for much.

Mrs. Garver had been most generous. Cassandra claimed to fear for taking a chill on their trip to the ice house—as well she should, of course, considering it was an ice house—and managed to get the woman to search out a wonderful assortment of warm clothes for her. She had her own coat and gloves back, all freshly cleaned, and also obtained some more practical boots along with a warm hat, a scarf, two woven shawls, and even woolen mittens. It was perfect. When time did come for her to make good her escape, she'd be well prepared for it.

She was not quite as prepared for seeing Papa, however. She found herself clutching at Lord Braden's arm for support when he led her into the ice house and up to the chilled block where Papa was laid. A more eerie setting could not have been had and it was all Cassandra could do to keep her legs steady as she walked up to the body.

"Will you... will you remove the shroud please, sir?" she asked Lord Braden in the strongest voice she could muster.

"Very well," he said.

And there was her father. His color was gone, except for his lips. They were now gray. His eyes remained closed and his expression was still passive, almost peaceful in fact, but his skin sagged in unusual places and his nose had become thin and his lips drawn apart. The father she had known was clearly gone away. This body was nothing more than a shell, just the mere remnant of what once had been.

The sadness of it all choked her and she put one mittened hand to her mouth trying to keep in the sob that struggled to come out. The hot tears stung when they spilled out of her eyes onto cold cheeks. As much as she ought to have hated this man for what he'd done—and for what he'd *not* done—over the years, she still loved him. Distant memories of life in the good days, before Mamma's death flooded back and she found she did not have to pretend to grieve. The pain was quite real. Everything that had been, everything that should have been, everything that never would be... it all washed over her and left her gasping for breath.

Lord Braden turned her away from the sight and pulled her into his arms. He had no idea what all she grieved just now, but she appreciated the comfort. Despite everything, it simply felt good to let herself get lost in the man's embrace. Just for a moment.

"We should go back now," he said when her body had ceased shaking and her breathing became regular again.

"No, please, let me stay. I need a moment with him. Alone."

She looked up at him, feeling her face go warm when his deep, dark eyes gazed back at her. It was time to give up this silly sentiment and get to work. She had a plan and needed to move on it, no matter how much she ached inside.

Swallowing back useless emotion, she took a deep breath and pushed away from him.

"Are you sure, Miss Horne?

"Yes. Thank you for coming out here with me, but if you don't mind, I really would like to be alone. Just for a while."

"Very well. I will wait just outside the entrance. Call for me if you need me."

"Thank you."

He left her. The air felt colder as his footsteps sounded in the confined chamber, echoing until he was outside the door. She shivered.

The ice house was little more than a cave carved into the side of a hill. It sat a fair distance from the castle, up on a slight ridge overlooking the icy stream that cut a jagged path through the land, looping around the castle to form a natural moat on three sides. Outside had been cold and gray, but here inside it was almost black and frigid. The lantern they had carried with them gave off only enough light to illuminate Papa where he lay, and cast macabre shadows over the mangled body of the coachman on a block a few feet away. She forced herself not to look. Even covered by a death shroud, she could tell that poor man had not met an easy end.

But now her task was at hand. She steeled herself and slipped out of the heavy mittens. Her fingers grew cold immediately, but she forced herself to set to work.

Papa hadn't mentioned exactly where he'd hidden the money in his clothing, so she prayed it was someplace easily accessible. She had no idea how she would explain herself if Lord Braden came back in to find her ransacking the beloved body. Gritting her teeth, she began feeling over Papa's arms, his chest, his sides, and... wait, there was something! In his coat, clearly something had been placed inside the lining near the bottom, just next to his arm. Indeed, he would have been able to easily feel for it to make sure it was still there.

She opened his coat, thankful it was ill-fitted and

left room for her to maneuver the material to the area she needed to investigate without having to do much to reposition Papa. She had remembered to take a knife from breakfast and pulled it out of her mitten now, using it to rip at the seams Papa had put in to conceal whatever he'd managed to bring. She could only hope it would be enough to meet her needs.

When a small leather pouch was finally revealed, she began to think perhaps it would be. It felt heavy as she eased it out of the lining and weighed it in her hands. How much had Papa brought? Where had he got it? Perhaps it would be best for her not to know.

Her gloved fingers fumbled at the string holding the pouch closed and she glanced over her shoulder to make sure Braden was not returning. There was no sign of him, the door to the ice house open, but his broad frame was not visible there. He was doing as he said, giving her time alone to grieve for her father. How could such a kind, honest man be in with the likes of Mr. Rovish? She simply could not understand the man.

But she did not need to understand him, she reminded herself. She needed to get away from him. She pulled the pouch open to reassure herself it did, indeed, contain money. It did. She did not take time to count it; she could ill afford to be caught with it.

Carefully so as not to jingle, she closed the pouch and slid it into her mitten along with the knife. She rearranged Papa's clothing, giving one last check to make sure there wasn't anything she might have overlooked. There wasn't. She pulled up the shroud and left him exactly the way she had found him. She slid her hands back into her mittens, clutching the pouch inside.

"Thank you, Papa," she whispered. "Maybe you finally did something right."

Leaving him, she pulled her coat tighter and grabbed up the lantern. Shadows danced along the walls and reflected through the many carved blocks of ice as she made her way to the door. She would not at all regret leaving this place.

"Do you feel better now?" Lord Braden asked, coming to attention where he had been leaning against the hewn rock that made up the facade of the cave.

Her smile was fragile, but she forced it. "Yes, I do, as a matter of fact."

"I'm happy to hear it. Now I am worried about keeping you out here. It's beginning to rain, I believe."

"Yes, it seems that it is. I'm afraid we'll both be quite wet by the time we get back indoors."

"Then we should hurry."

She agreed, trotting along beside him. The rain began as nothing more than a drizzle, but it soon turned to honest droplets that increased in size and determination to drench them. They were making their way along a path that followed the stream, but the castle still loomed far ahead of them. She should not have taken so long in the ice house, she supposed.

As the wind picked up, blowing tiny bits of ice along with the rain, she truly regretted spending any time at all in the ice house. She was not yet fully recovered from all her aches and bruises from the accident, and certainly the ache in her soul was cavernous and cold. This freezing rain that soaked into her bones made everything worse. Her teeth began to chatter and she stumbled over her own numb feet.

"Come here," Lord Braden said, pulling her to a

stop beneath the relative shelter of a towering evergreen.

She was going to argue, but he quickly unbuttoned his coat and pulled it open, wrapping it around her as he held her against him. The warmth from his body flooded her and suddenly she did not want to argue at all. She wanted to stay with him forever.

"You're half frozen," he said. "I've got to get you inside."

She was shaking so hard she couldn't quite form the words to reply. Her reply came out a weak little mumble. Her legs went suddenly weak, as well.

"Oh, hell," he murmured.

Without so much as an effort her scooped her up into his arms and continued on toward the castle. He was carrying her! Heavens, what an unusual sensation. Is this how he had brought her here in the first place? Pity she had been unconscious for it.

She wrapped her arms around his neck and was quite pleased to be awake this time.

If the man grew tired from carrying her he never did show it. She tucked her face against his shoulder to hide from the rain, but also to absorb more of the heat from his body. He seemed to have plenty of it, even though he felt almost solid as rock. When he suddenly stopped moving and set her down onto her feet she was really quite bereft.

They had arrived at the nearest door. Servants inside came rushing out to meet them and he bustled her indoors. Apparently this door led to the kitchen. The fire was roaring yet not nearly so warm as the heat she'd felt pressed up against him. She was glad for all the rushing about, finding blankets and dry things for them. It allowed her to avoid meeting his eyes, or giving away the fact that the rose in her cheeks was hardly due to the wind or the rain.

Mrs. Garver hovered over her, rubbing her with towels and clicking her tongue in disapproval.

"Dreadful weather out there. Not fit for you at all. Here my dear, let me get you up to your room."

Tremors ran through her in waves and she fisted her hand around the precious money pouch. She let Mrs. Garver lead her way but could not deny herself one last glance over at Braden. He watched her with dark, storming eyes. He was angry at her.

She could hardly blame him. His clothes were a mess and his hair dripped with rivulets. No doubt he was as cold as she and his back probably hurt from hauling her like luggage again.

"I'm sorry I took you out into the rain, sir."

"I should not have allowed it."

"But I'm glad that you did. Thank you."

"You may thank me when I'm convinced you haven't got pneumonia."

There was no time to reply. Mrs. Garver had her in hand and was calling for a maid to assist. Hot water for a bath was already being summoned as were more towels and heated blankets. She could do little but let herself be led away. As they filed out the door she got one last glimpse of Braden, watching after her as he warmed his hands by the fire. His coat was removed and his wet shirt plastered against his sturdy form.

How on earth could a man so windblown and so bedraggled look so terribly handsome? And how could she suddenly be so very warm after coming in from that blast?

Chapter 9

"So the physician is unavailable?" Braden asked, hoping he'd heard wrong.

"I'm sorry," Drake replied. "That's what the boy that I sent to the village said. Seems Dr. Lowe is out treating some plague in the next county. The nearest physician aside from him is probably a full day's ride away."

"Damn. What if Miss Horne takes a turn? What if she doesn't have a full day or two to wait for some other physician to get here?"

"I'm sure she'll be fine."

"You didn't see her, man. She was like ice, her face all gone pale and the trembling nearly over took her. She wasn't yet recovered from her last encounter with our wretched elements, yet I dragged her out into it. No, we need someone to come straight away and see that she is well cared for."

"Mrs. Garver will see that she—"

"Mrs. Garver is not a physician! I need someone with a trained medical background to be here, to watch for the earliest signs of any sort— what the devil are you laughing at, Drake?"

"You, sir."

"And what the bloody hell do you find so very funny about me?"

"I never thought to see you like this, sir."

"Like what, damn it?"

"In love, obviously."

"In *what*?"

"Somehow you've fallen in love with Miss Horne."

"Don't be ridiculous. Just because I don't want the girl to die of an ague or something putrid doesn't mean I've... er..."

"You can't even say it, can you? Oh, but this is rich. You railed on and on about what a horror she seemed, and now you've gone and bloody fallen in love with her."

"You'll do well to watch how you talk, Drake."

"She is a pretty thing, I'll give you that."

"Watch how you talk, Drake."

"But what of her dislike of animals? Her determination to drag you away from MacMorton?"

"She doesn't so much dislike animals. She's tolerated them rather well, I should say. And twice now she's asked me to show her around the place. She claims to find my home fascinating."

"Probably wondering what goods you have she can take back to London and sell."

"That's enough! You may be more like a brother to me than just my hired man, but I won't have you discuss her. Miss Horne is none of your business, Drake."

"Because you're the one in love with her."

"I'm the one damn well going to marry her."

"And I couldn't be happier for you, my lord. Especially since you've gone completely soft in the head over her."

Braden bit back some not very polite words. They

would have been a waste of breath, at any rate. It seemed Drake was correct. Clearly he *had* gone soft in the head. He'd given in to Miss Horne's sentimental pleading, her fluttering lashes and her rosebud-like lips. She asked to go see her father's body, and he'd tossed good sense out the window. He'd taken her, and in the process he'd put her in danger of catching her death. By God, if he had to lay *her* out in that ice house...

Damn it to hell, but Drake *was* correct. He had fallen in love with the girl. How could that have happened? Before he found her lying in that heap of tangled carriage he'd not had one drop of warmth for her. How had he managed to lose his heart to her in such a short time? It didn't seem possible.

But obviously it was. She filled his thoughts whether he liked it or not. Just a few days ago he thought the worst fate imaginable would be losing MacMorton Castle and the lands that he loved so dearly. Today, though, he could think of nothing worse than losing *her*, or watching her suffer. It was not sensible.

No wonder Drake had been laughing at him.

"I'll send someone out to find another physician, my lord," his faithful steward assured him.

"Send a groom, not just a boy. Use my fastest horse."

"You sold your fastest horse, sir. Remember? To old Mr. Rovish. He paid more than it's worth, too."

"I like that horse, Drake. It's still here, isn't it?"

"It is, actually. Rovish said his son would be traveling home to spend Christmas and he'd send him to pick it up then."

"Well, he's not shown up for it yet, so your man can

still use it. Send him now."

"Rovish likely won't like that, seeing as he's already paid."

"I intend to buy the horse back just as soon as I'm able, so go ahead and send him."

"But the roads, sir..."

"Yes, the roads are bad for a carriage. A rider will get through."

Drake sighed and gave up. "Very well, sir. Let's just hope the physician we find has a sturdy horse of his own."

"Send one with your rider. Surely we haven't sold all of the horses yet, have we?"

"I'll find something. In the meanwhile, don't worry about the young miss. I think she's stronger than she seems."

"I hope not," he muttered mostly to himself as Drake headed out to work a miracle.

If Miss Horne was too strong, she might realize she did not need a penniless earl with a crumbling castle and nothing else to offer. He rather hoped she might not see that. He hoped, in fact, he might find some part of her just vulnerable enough to perhaps need him the tiniest bit.

Mrs. Garver assured her she had everything she needed, but Cassandra was not convinced. True, her room was toasty warm and she'd been given a fresh set of clothing, and yes, she'd managed to get that money off Papa's body and hide it under her bed, but still she felt restless. She'd been told to get rest, but her body simply would not comply. She was nervous and jumpy, unable to relax.

She tried to settle on plotting her escape, but her mind just wouldn't cooperate. It was as if a large part of her was actually resistant to the idea of leaving. What insanity was that? Perhaps she had indeed taken a chill and it affected her brain.

She wanted to go, had actually seen a fair bit of the castle when she and Lord Braden had made their way out of it and then even more when they made their way back in. She'd been through servant's rooms and seen one or two areas—with external doors—that appeared rarely used. It was still early in the day. There should be no reason for her not to make good on her plans.

Except that she simply could not make herself leave. She tried to tell herself it was because she hadn't yet worked out that detail of transportation. Indeed, that was quite an important, detail, too. But she had overheard a maid telling the men who brought up the bath that there would be Christmas festivities in the village. There was too much bustle at the time for Cassandra to ask exactly what village she meant, but surely it must be close by. If there was a village, then surely she could get to it and find a way home.

If only her feet would comply with her brain's decision to go. If only her brain would finally make that decision. For now, though, it seemed pacing her room was all any part of her could agree on.

She jumped when a knock came at her door. Likely it was Mrs. Garver bringing her tea or an additional blanket or a girl with more coal for the grate. Instead, though, she opened the door to find Lord Braden with kittens.

"I promised to bring these little fellows to see you. I

hope you don't mind."

"Mind? Heavens no! Come in!"

She opened the door wide to allow him in with the basket full of wriggling, mewing, wide-eyed fluff. He placed the basket gently on the floor. His hair had dried, but still flopped about his head as if it were not quite sure how to right itself after their adventure. She would have very much liked to get her hands in it to give guidance. Also, she tried not to recall the warmth of his body or the way his shirt fit tight over him when it had been soaked through with rain. And how he had smelled like pine and fresh linen.

Drat. Now her face had gone hot again.

"Forgive my intrusion," he said, herding the kittens back into the basket as they tumbled out in all directions. "But I had to see for myself that you were quite well, even after I'd let you half drown."

"You let me? It was my idea to go out there, my lord. I should apologize to you, after all."

"Nonsense. It was only natural you would wish to see your father. I should have taken more care to protect you from the weather."

"You carried me, sir. I should say that is making more than an extra effort."

"Forgive me. Such forward behavior must have been quite shocking to you."

Had her face already been warm? Now it was burning. She supposed he was correct; a proper lady should indeed have been quite shocked getting whisked of her feet in that manner. She had not been. She rather had liked it.

"You were most kind, sir. But I worry after taking on such a burden you might find yourself in need of doctoring for your overtaxed back."

He actually laughed at that. "You're hardly a burden, Miss Horne. But as you mention a doctor, I ought to tell you I've sent a man off to bring back a physician."

"Whatever for?"

"For you, of course. You had some very nasty bruises. The roads are improved enough to send out a rider and with luck he'll bring a man back."

"Truly, you don't need to go to all that trouble for me! I'm quite well now, as you can see."

"Indeed, you do look well."

His appraising gaze indicated he meant his words in all earnest. She lowered her eyes and dropped down to her knees beside the rolling and pouncing kittens. How could she let him affect her like this? She was preparing to escape the man, for heaven's sake. She should most definitely not be grinning like a giddy girl under his watchful eyes.

"I have no need of a doctor," she insisted. "Your man need not put himself out."

"It's too late. He's already off. Besides, we've learned that our local physician is away treating an epidemic. It seems we're in luck, though. I've just heard there is a physician from London passing nearby."

"Physician from London?"

"Indeed. I thought perhaps you might know him, or at least you could send word back with him of what has transpired. No doubt we should discuss getting word to your family."

"Er, yes... I might know him."

Good heavens, what if she did? Grandmother kept all manner of medical persons dancing to her tune whenever they were in Town. She claimed her delicate constitution required it, but of course Cassandra knew the dear woman just loved the attention. It was not at all unreasonable to think that this London physician might at some time have encountered them on one of their infrequent visits.

Or worse, perhaps this man knew the real Miss Horne! Gracious, how would she work around that one? Clearly she could not afford to be here when the man arrived. She'd have to make very, very certain her escape went as intended. Between doctors and Rovish and Lord Braden's plan to hide her in the dungeon, everything hinged on getting out of here. Now.

"I suppose London is a big place, though," he said. "It is very improbable that you should know the man. But I thought it might comfort you to at least meet with someone from your own town. And *I* would be much comforted to know you've suffered no lasting harm."

"That's very kind of you, sir. And it was kind of you to bring me these kittens. They are adorable, aren't they?"

"Indeed. Not a mouse in the castle will be safe once they've learned to walk without tripping over themselves."

"I hope the mice aren't watching them now."

They'd likely be laughing their stringy gray tails off. It was dreadfully cute the way these little monsters were hopping and stalking without anything close to the agility of an actually cat. They ran into one another, they chased their own tails, they cowered in pretend terror at dust motes and shadows. If things were not quite so dire, she'd love nothing more than to sit watching them for hours, perhaps locate a ball of yarn...

But things were dire. She must keep her mind focused.

"I promise, Miss Horne, there are no mice in your room."

"Indeed I'm glad for that, sir. But what of the rest of the castle? You know you promised to show it to me today."

"Indeed I did. Are you certain you feel up to that?"

"I do, my lord. I've been quite eager for it, as a matter of fact."

"Have you? Well, then. I should not like to disappoint. I will take my leave and instruct Mrs. Garver that after you have had some sort of meal to assure your well-being, you and I shall meet for a grand—yet not over-exerting—tour of my castle."

He had crouched down to dangle his fingers for a kitten to bat. His gaze left the kitten now and her eyes met his. He felt inordinately close, although truly he was on the opposite side of the basket. Still, she fancied she could feel the heat radiate from his body and breathe in his scent even from here, where she sat on the floor.

"Thank you, my lord," she replied, wishing her voice had not played her so false and gone all breathy and soft.

At breakfast she'd been actually trying to ply him with sweetness. Just now she had not. This odd tone to her voice must be earnest.

He did not seem to mind her voice, though. He teased at the kitten for a minute or two more, then cleared his throat and stood up to full height. It seemed as if he towered over her, made her feel small. She worried that this thought did not fill her with fear of the man, even with all that she knew of him and his schemes. Something about Lord Braden begged her to trust.

She wouldn't.

"Until then, my dear Miss Horne," he said.

She gave a polite nod and a cool "good day" which left him with nothing to do but bow and remove himself from the room. Her spine went slack when the door shut behind him. The kittens ignored her, choosing now to discover the edge of the coverlet hanging over the bed, and she watched them with only half an interest. If only she could enjoy her surroundings with such carefree abandon as they were.

Indeed, she truly wanted to. If she were honest with herself, she'd admit she was looking forward to her tour of his castle. She was looking forward to it too much, and for all the wrong reasons. Oh, but the sooner she left here the better it would be for all of them.

"Send that back to the kitchen and let the staff enjoy it," Braden announced when a cold tray was brought into his office.

"But sir, you hardly touched your breakfast," Mrs. Garver complained, hovering over the timid maid who carried the tray. "You have to eat something."

"Was food taken up to Miss Horne?"

"Yes, yes, and she was a very good girl and actually ate it."

"Excellent. Then I suppose I should meet her now and show her around the castle as we have planned. Is everyone ready for that?"

The housekeeper sighed as if the whole thing were

far too much work, but Braden was not blind to the smile that hinted at the corner of her eyes. The woman tried to be a starchy sergeant at arms, directing all that occurred here with smug firmness, but Braden knew better. Mrs. Garver had a heart of gold beneath the granite exterior she tried to display.

"We are ready, sir," she replied. "The servants have been instructed to look busy, to be cheerful, and to do everything possible to make the place look... thriving."

"Very good. Thank you, Mrs. Garver. You are indispensible, you know."

"Indeed, sir. And... if you would please keep the young lady out of the some of the more, er, questionable areas?"

"You mean where there is a chance she might fall through the floor or suffer the roof caving in on us? Yes, Mrs. Garver. We will avoid those parts of the castle."

"Well then. I've certain done all I can, my lord. I suppose the rest is up to you."

The girl with the tray hid back a giggle. Braden knew the household must spend long hours debating his ability to get Miss Horne off to the altar. It was no secret—despite his many efforts to keep it so—that everything hinged on his capacity to sway and to charm the grieving young woman. He hoped he would not disappoint.

"Why Mrs. Garver, you sound as if you doubt my abilities. I assure you, Miss Horne is proving to be far more agreeable than I ever imagined. Now, take away this tray and concentrate on the areas where you might entice Miss Horn. I'll concentrate on mine."

The young servant giggled again and Mrs. Garver

looked as if she might wish to dispute his pretense of confidence, but in the end she gave a broad nod.

"Very well, sir. Come, Sally, let us go appear warm and well fed."

He chuckled as they scurried off. She'd been funning him, of course. His servants never went hungry, not yet anyway. They were a bit on the cool side, he supposed, as fuel for the fires was lately very scarce, but he'd never yet stopped feeding them all. If this day with Miss Horne went well, it would be safe to presume the issue of heat would soon be resolved, too. The Horne money could pay for a wagon load of coal, delivered each day, if they wanted. He merely had to charm the girl and convince her to give her vows and sign in the ledger.

So far the charming part seemed to be going quite well. He'd hardly had to work at it, finding her pleasant and engaging apparently by nature. Of course it must be a fluke and a symptom of her ordeal, but if he could just keep her this way for one day more... Yes, at this rate, that was all he might need. By this time tomorrow, they might be seeing the parson.

His wedding. And to think, he'd been dreading the day. Miss Horne had certainly been a delightful surprise.

Chapter 10

"It's lovely!" Cassandra exclaimed when Lord Braden swept open the doors to a remarkably spacious ballroom.

"This room is a newer addition to the castle," he explained, leading her into the ornately painted ballroom with tall columns and a wide marble floor. "My grandfather put it in to impress the few people who ever did come to visit. Unfortunately, no one ever visits so the room has seen very little use."

She'd been thrilled with the history of the building he'd been telling her, of the ancient squires and lords who had called the place home, the battles it had withstood and the villagers it had protected. Some of the age was quite obvious, of course, and she couldn't help wonder how such a castle might have looked when it was pristine, or at least fully decked in festive display.

As it was, this room showed just the barest of attention to holiday trimmings.

"Your servants are very industrious," she noted. "Even in such an unused room they began to carefully decorate."

"Er, yes. They seem to enjoy making the place merry."

"Pity you told them to stop. Such a lovely space—it ought to be decorated."

He shrugged. "Perhaps in London you decorate rooms you don't use. Here in the country we tend to be a bit more practical."

"I just think it's a pity you don't find reason to use the room. I would think MacMorton castle a perfect place for hosting holidays, or hunting parties, or... why do you make that face?"

"What? Forgive me, Miss Horne. I'll admit I'm rather an embarrassment to my peers. Hunting, you see, has never been one of my favorite pastimes. I find the idea distasteful, I'm afraid."

Her face likely showed her surprise. Lord Braden amazed her. What a refreshing thing, to find a titled gentleman who did not choose to participate in a noisesome, cruel, and often dangerous activity *and* who was not ashamed to say so. She could quite see that a man who rescued badgers and twiddled his fingers for kittens might not wish to storm out to dispatch a poor fox. She rather liked this about him.

Of course, she mustn't let herself be distracted. She had heard him conspiring with his man. He might not hunt animals, but he certainly had no qualms about abducting ladies. She needed to keep her mind on her task, and her task at this moment was to study this castle.

Clearly he'd been showing her the expected things; rooms with fine furnishing, halls to host banquets and areas bustling with happy servants. She did not fail to notice, however, that in all of these rooms—flawlessly tidy, as they were—the draperies showed signs of wear, the carpets were torn, and the wall hangings suffered decay and some thread loss. In certain rooms she detected walls and floors that indicated uneven fading and open spaces. Most likely they had at one time been covered by items that had recently been removed.

Had Lord Braden been rearranging? For the holiday, perhaps. The servants had taken great pains, it appeared, to fill these open spaces with greenery and pinecones and holly and other sweetly scented things that made the whole castle smell festive and cheery. Warm fires burned only in certain rooms, as if he had orchestrated this tour to put the place in the best possible light. She wondered at that, why he'd worked to make some parts so very inviting.

What she needed, of course, was to visit the less inviting areas. She let him lead her from the half-decorated ballroom. He turned toward the right, so she turned to the left and meandered down a long chilly corridor that turned into a wide gallery. He followed, not calling her back, but not noticeably happy she had strayed. All the more reason, she thought, to investigate.

"This gallery feels very old," she said, glancing around.

The place was clearly medieval, with thick stone walls and tall, narrow windows all along one side. A huge fireplace—large enough for her to stand in—occupied the entirety of the other long wall. She was vaguely surprised not to find rows of armored suits flanking them. No antlers or busts of dead animals, either. It was curiously empty.

"It is old. This is part of the original keep, built by my ancestors and used to sign treaties, greet guests and... arrange marriages."

"I see," she said, feeling an involuntary chill at the mention of marriage.

She studied the gallery, taking a turn and admiring everything from the cold stone walls to the dark wood of the vaulted ceiling. She noticed the huge, carved doors at the opposite end of the gallery.

"So would those open to the oldest parts of the castle?"

He didn't answer directly but took a moment to draw a deep breath and contemplate his reply. "There are a few areas that have fallen to disuse. I do not generally go to the older parts of the castle."

She found that hard to believe. The man loved this place. She could not quite imagine him ignoring a large portion of it. What was he hiding?

He likely wouldn't tell her, of course, but she could see how he reacted to questions.

"What is in the older part of the castle, the areas you do not use?"

"Er, very little of interest. Dark, dusty places. A crumbling tower, the dungeons—"

"Dungeons? Were they used to house prisoners?"

"Er, what?"

"How were they used?"

Again, his answer was delayed and his gaze flitted about the room, his eyes not meeting hers. She thought this quite telling.

"Possibly for prisoners in the past. Now it is merely used for occasional storage, of course. I harbor no implements of torture or dark, forgotten cells."

Well, that was encouraging. If it could be believed.

"Truly? I'd very much like to see that," she said, trying to sound like nothing more than a young woman in search of diversion rather than someone seeking privileged knowledge.

"You would? It is hardly the finest part of the castle."

"Oh, but it is exciting... like something from a tale of adventure and romance."

Now his eyes did latch onto her hers. She worried perhaps she'd shown a bit too much interest in his dungeon, but thankfully he smiled.

"So you are a reader of novels, are you, Miss Horne?"

"I am guilty of that, sir. I fear I do love to sit over my candle until late after dark, shuddering in horror at the fate of some poor heroine. Please, if you have dungeons I must take a look at them!"

"Oh, very well. How can I deny you such rapturous pleasure?"

He laughed at the silliness of it, but she was glad to have fooled him. Clearly he thought her nothing more than a cotton-headed female a fair bit too fond of the Minerva Press. Fine. It was just as she needed.

"But please keep near to me, Miss Horne. I'd prefer not to lose you in the labyrinth of horrors below MacMorton Castle."

"Er, I thought you said it was little more than storage these days, sir?"

He laughed again. "I did, Miss Horne. You will be perfectly safe. I merely thought it a fair opportunity to keep you near to me."

If he'd been hoping to make her blush over that, he was probably quite pleased. She felt the heat rising and knew her face had gone pink. The man was a charmer, she'd give him full marks. Whether or not he was a kidnapper remained to be seen. Hopefully, she would not be here to see.

It was actually quite brilliant to bring the woman down here. Braden carried the lantern while shadows and spiders and tiny little footsteps scurried all around them. The low ceilings and long, narrow corridors of the maze-like lower levels made it feel as if they were miles away from anyone and really quite at risk.

He, of course, had prowled these places since childhood and knew them quite well, but obviously Miss Horne did not. She clung to his arm, pressing her body against him and jumping at every odd sound or strange outline that loomed before them in the darkness. Yet she did not beg him to return her to the ground floor, so he continued on, leading her deeper into the abyss.

"I'm told that during Cromwell's rule this area was sealed off and used to hide all manner of weapons, my family being secretly loyal to the crown," he explained.

"Truly? You must be very proud of your family."

The distant ones, perhaps. There had been men of great conscience that came here before him. More recently, however, the lords Braden had been more interested in bankrupting the estate than putting their efforts into anything more meaningful. He could hardly admit to being proud of that.

And he certainly would not admit any of it to Miss Horne. She wanted a fine title and that's what he would give her. He hoped it might be years before she found it was tarnished by debauchery, cruelty and sloth.

"I'm sure your family has many interesting stories

from the past," he said, redirecting her focus. "After all, your father cannot have made such a success of himself without some measure of struggle. His merchant vessels must be very grand. Have you sailed with him?"

He couldn't make out her expression in the dim light, but he could feel how her body went stiff. Her voice came out tight and brittle when she answered.

"Er, no. Have I given you the impression that I have?"

"No, as a matter of fact, I don't recall the subject coming up in our correspondence. That's why I thought to ask of it now. Indeed, I am eager to know very much more about you, my dear."

Apparently she was not eager to tell him. She swiftly made some redirection of her own.

"Look, a very sturdy door. Where do you suppose that leads?"

"That? I'm sure you'd love to hear that it leads to some secret chamber were all manner of gruesome tortures were performed on heretics, false lovers or rogues, but I'm sorry to say it is merely a door to the surface."

"You mean it leads out?"

"It does."

"Oh. I do not see a lock."

Indeed, she was far too used to living in Town with footpads and burglars around every corner. He patted her hand and assured her.

"Don't fear. This castle has not faced any onslaught in centuries. My servants are watchful and will keep us safe."

"So you mean... this door is open for anyone to come or go as they please?"

"Of course, should it please anyone to come or go through my dungeon. So far as I know, my dear, no one ever does."

He hadn't tried it in years. In fact, he found it likely to assume that the hinges on the door might be rusted in place. Or perhaps the wood had gone rotten and the whole thing would crumble to splinters should anyone try to use it. It might be best to keep her going, away from the door, as a matter of fact.

"Now over here, if you look, you can see what's left of the old casks used for holding the ale that kept everyone in high spirits. We have newer ones now in another area."

Newer and much smaller, unfortunately.

"It is quite confusing down here," she said. "I'm beginning to worry we shall not find our way out."

"I know my own home, Miss Horne, so never you fear."

She said nothing more. He waited a heartbeat then continued.

"I hope someday you will know it so well, too."

"I should like that," she said softly.

Just what he'd been hoping to hear! They'd done as he wished. He and his servants had made MacMorton so inviting, so warm and so comfortable that she'd overlooked the drafty walls, the worn furnishings, the fact that he could barely afford to heat even the most common of rooms. She approved of his home.

"Then dare I hope that MacMorton will, in fact, soon be your home?"

He held his breath, waiting for her answer.

"Er, it is rather cool down here, isn't it?"

"Dungeons often are, so it seems."

"Perhaps we should go up."

"Why, Miss Horne? To escape the cold, or to escape me?"

She shifted away from him. He took her by the shoulder and held the lantern down so they could meet one another's gaze without glare. She was hesitant, but finally looked up at him.

"Why should I have need to escape you, my lord?" she asked.

He knew what she meant. She'd made her position clear from the start. She did not wish to remain here for life. The fact that she'd not complained about everything she'd encountered since her arrival was to her great credit, but of course he could hardly expect it to mean more than that she had been gracious. She had made very clear what her plans were for their future. MacMorton played little role in them, unfortunately.

He would be man enough to accept this.

"You have no need to escape me, Miss Horne. I will honor our arrangement as planned."

"Er... I'm happy to hear of it, sir."

"I hope I'd not given you reason to doubt."

"No... no reason, my lord. No reason at all. What reason could I possibly have?"

She was studying him closely, rubbing her hands over her arms. He noticed she shivered. The poor thing. She was not at all easy with their situation, he could see that. Perhaps it was the shadows and the damp. Perhaps it was losing her father. Perhaps it was him.

She must have realized that with her father gone she was more or less at his mercy. Once they were married, he would control her money, her comings and goings; her very life. No doubt she would fear he might not be a man of his word. What a worrisome position she must find herself in. He should relieve some of that worry.

"When I am your husband, my dear, you shall be allowed everything that ensures your happiness."

"Truly?" Her face showed she found this difficult to believe.

"Of course. Should you want to leave this place, you have only to ask."

"Once we are married you will let me leave?"

"I have promised you that is what I will do."

"But until then?"

"Until then? Well, that's rather the point we need to discuss, isn't it?"

"Er, yes, I suppose it is."

"So, you are not convinced that you wish to marry right away? Of course I can certainly understand your feelings on this. The accident, and your father's loss... it hardly seems proper to celebrate a wedding so soon after all of that."

He waited a moment for her to speak, but she did not. So he went on.

"But the roads are not good, my dear. A lone rider might get through—I am hoping he will—but I am loathe to trust your safety in travel. That leaves you stranded here, without the benefit of your father or even a chaperone. Truly, you must see the awkwardness of the situation."

"Awkwardness?"

"If we were to wait until the roads are clean and then travel together to London... and arrive there not as man and wife... well, you can imagine the scandal that might invite. I would never expose you to such a thing."

"So what are you suggesting, sir?"

"Marry me, Miss Horne. Marry me now."

"Now?"

"No, not this very moment, of course. But tomorrow. I have the license, the parson is near. We can be married without delay and then travel to London at our leisure, when your safety—and your reputation— can be assured."

"You have given this some thought, it appears."

"I have. And may I encourage you to think on it, as well?"

"And if I decide I cannot agree to it?"

He was afraid of that. He had pushed too hard, been too insensitive to her pain. It was too soon to pressure her into this and he'd known it. Only his selfish motives had spurred him on to demand of her what any female with a heart would clearly find impossible.

"If you cannot agree to it, Miss Horne, then we are faced with a problem, aren't we?"

Indeed, it seemed there would be a problem. The hair rose at the back of Cassandra's neck and she glanced around the dark corridors and eerie passages. Not a comforting place, to say the least.

Lord Braden was making it very clear that he fully intended to wed on the morrow. He'd painted a rather dismal picture for his intended, a picture that could only be made brighter by compliance with his plan. She wondered what he might do if she refused. Was his plan to lock her down here in league with Mr. Rovish already in motion, or had he been waiting to try to sway her with gentler means? If she agreed with the man now, would he forgo anything further, considering himself assured of his wife?

Good sense urged her to be compliant. But complying meant agreeing, and how on earth could she agree to marry the man? She had no intention of it! Indeed, it wasn't really *her* he was asking. He thought she was Miss Horne. *Miss Horne* was the woman he'd come to know, to care for through correspondence. He would likely not take it well when he found out the truth.

Then again, she very much did not like the idea of being locked down here should she not agree. She had plotted her escape and all she needed was time. Time could be gained by making Lord Braden think he had no reason to worry. He needed to trust her, to let down his guard. To believe he had won. Therefore, a lie was the only logical course.

"Of course I will marry you, sir. Whenever you think is best."

They had been easy words to say. Meeting his eyes after saying them had not. But she forced herself and was immediately held captive.

His expression confused her. Yet what could be confusing about the man's smile, or the warm light that shone in his eyes? The confusion, obviously, came from her own conflicted emotion. She'd done as she hoped, she'd distracted him with her supposed consent. He trusted he now. Why should she not be giddy with pride and pleased with her accomplishment?

Because some part of her couldn't quite believe he was evil. Some part of her raced at the sight of his smile, the longing in his eyes. Some part of her wanted to ignore everything she knew to be true about him.

"I am the happiest of men," he said tenderly,

stroking her cheek and gazing at her as if she were some grand prize.

Oh, but she believed the man. He truly did look happy. He must honestly care for Miss Horne in a very real, very deep way. He could never be capable of what she suspected.

But she had heard him! Oh, what was wrong with her brain? How could she trust what she felt and discount what she'd seen? She couldn't. She simply must get her mind off his sweet tone, his gentle touch, his earnest expression or those deep, soulful eyes. As well as any other part of him.

"Perhaps we should go back upstairs now?" she said.

He seemed to think she was funning. "Surely you can't be worried for taking a chill, my dear. By that adorable glow in your cheeks you appear rather warm."

"I... er, I do feel rather a chill."

"Then I will correct that problem for you."

He did so right away, actually, by pulling her into his arms. She was too surprised to react. Heavens, but he was very warm, indeed! In fact, without the benefit of wind and rain to cool things off, she was just a bit concerned he might, in fact, be too hot.

Certainly she was.

Chapter 11

She was just the perfect little bundle in his arms, soft and round in all the right places. And she'd agreed to marry him as early as possible! It was nearly too good to be true. Could it be that she'd been just as pleased with him as he had with her?

He'd learned years ago not to expect miracles, yet this was beginning to feel like one. Certainly only an angel brought miracles, and Miss Horne certainly felt like an angel. The hope that perhaps they might even be happy with one another went a very long way toward making him feel like less of a devil.

She'd agreed to marry him, yes, but only after he'd painted a very bleak picture for her. It was truly unfair for him to do that, he knew, but desperation had taken over. Plus something a bit more... something not quite driven so much by his need to save his castle as it was a need for...

Her. He needed *her*. Not just any wife, but this one... this particular woman. It seemed amazing now to think of how he'd not seen in her letters what she really was. He must have resented the notion that he must marry for money so very strongly that it tainted his opinion of her. He'd clearly misinterpreted her words all along. Thank heavens he knew the truth now.

Miss Horne was everything he'd ever dreamed of. And more. He pulled her closer and leaned in to taste those cherry lips he'd been admiring for three days.

She stopped him.

"Wait, my lord."

"What is it, my dear?"

She was shy. How darling. She likely needed just a bit more coaxing to woo her tender sensibilities.

"Er... you have a spider on your shoulder."

"A what?"

"I'll get it."

Without further concern for her own wellbeing, she reached up and brushed the spindly-legged creature off of Braden's coat. He stared in wonder as she did not scream nor swoon nor run off in terror. She simply batted her eyes and gave a nervous smile.

"I'm sorry. Had you wanted to keep that one, sir?"

My God. An angel, indeed.

"Miss Horne, or may I say, Philberta, I must tell you that I—"

"Philberta?"

"May I not call you by your given name?"

"Er, I suppose so, but... my name is Philberta?"

"Philberta Horne. I do have that correct, don't I?"

"Oh, yes of course. I just... it sounds so strange coming from you, my lord."

"And is it too strange to ask that you call me by my given name? I've heard it is customary for engaged couples to do so."

She did indeed seem disconcerted by this notion. Again, he thought it was darling. For an elegant young woman of London to be so unassuming now that he had her here in his arms, he found that quite a surprise.

Everything about Miss Horne surprised him. He liked that.

"I'm not sure I can do that, my lord, I..."

"Crowley. I call you Philberta and you call me Crowley."

What was that odd expression on her face. It was almost as if he had surprised her. Well, he could only hope he had done so and she'd found it every bit as delightful as the surprises she'd given him.

"Gracious. I'll certainly try to remember that," she said, almost as if to herself.

He decided they'd bantered enough. The air here was cool and this woman needed warming. He intended to do just that.

Unfortunately, she startled at the sudden sound of approaching footsteps. Heavy, labored footsteps, from what he could tell. Damn the interruption.

"Have you come seeking me, Drake?" he called out as soon as his man became visible in the darkness.

Now Drake seemed to startle. He'd been hefting a large crate and dropped it as the light from Braden's lantern reached him at the far end of the corridor. The contents of the crate—chains, by the sound of it— rattled jarringly.

"Oh... I'm sorry, my lord. Didn't know you were down here."

"But you came looking for me."

He could not let Miss Horne guess what real purpose Drake had for being down here, for making the place ready to host stolen goods. He hoped Drake would be discreet.

"Oh, er... yes, my lord. I came looking for you. What I meant was, I didn't know you had Miss Horne down here with you. Didn't mean to interrupt anything."

"You didn't, Drake." *Not yet, anyway.*

"Good, then. I was just looking for you to, er, now why was I here looking for you?"

"I imagine you wanted to tell me you'd been checking the coal supplies. We store them down here, I believe."

"We do... that's it! I've been checking the coal supplies."

"And what did you find?"

"Er... did I find anything, sir?"

"I suppose you found that everything is as it should be."

"Yes. Exactly that. I'm happy to report it."

"Excellent, Drake."

They stood there, Drake looking guilty as he hovered over his crate of chain, Miss Horne blinking in confusion and nervously righting her clothing as if she did, indeed, have some reason for them to be out of order. Braden just wondered how better to explain his steward's sudden and awkward arrival down here. Since he could not come up with anything more plausible than coal, perhaps retreat was in order.

"Very well then," he said, taking Miss Horne's arm since she'd so hurriedly pried herself out of his embrace. "Continue, Drake. We will be returning to more hospitable rooms."

Drake mumbled something, but stood where he was. Braden nodded at him, raised his lantern, then led Miss Horne up an adjoining corridor. This was not the most direct route back up to their living quarters, but it would keep them out of the area where Drake was working to set up a place for the foxes that would be, for better or for worse, joining them here tonight.

The less Miss Horne saw of those preparations, the better. Things were going so well between them, Braded did not wish for any little thing that might tip the apple cart. Or enlighten Miss Horne as to the sort of man she was actually going to end up with. He'd much rather she held to the illusion of dignified nobility that he'd tried so very hard to present.

It was what she wanted, after all. And he wanted her. Perhaps after enough time passed he might actually become the very man he pretended to be. Then surely his conscience wouldn't nag at him so.

Who knew, he might even come to love London. After finding Miss Horne, he was beginning to believe anything was possible. If only he could believe hiding a dozen wild foxes in his dungeon would prove uneventful.

She knew exactly what was going on in Lord Braden's dungeon. He was preparing to hold her there if she so much as hinted that she might change her mind regarding their wedding. Thank heavens they'd been interrupted before she'd been completely duped by his false kindness and those dratted nice eyes. That wandering servant likely had saved her.

No wonder the earl had stammered and tried to put words in his servant's mouth. He was hiding the fact that the man was hauling a crate full of chains. And to think, she'd been about to let Lord Braden kiss her! As if she really did intend to end up married to him.

Oh, but this was dreadful. She had more than enough proof to convince herself of his guilt, yet she just could not reconcile it. He did not seem evil—not at all. She had wanted to kiss him!

Well, there would be no kisses. Once she was safely upstairs she would thank him for his time, then claim a headache. Or a chill. Or simple fatigue. Or all of them. He did, after all, keep reminding her of the ordeal she'd so recently been through. Surely he'd not think it amiss if she spent the rest of the day in her room and then skipped having dinner.

Or would he? She'd just agreed to marry the man. It might be reasonable to expect he was looking forward to dining together, to discussing their plans and making arrangements. It would probably seem odd, in fact, if she were not eager for that, as well. If she didn't show up for dinner, he'd probably come looking for her. Even though she'd paid close attention during their tour, she had no doubt he might find her. He knew MacMorton's hiding places far better than she.

What she needed was a head start. She needed to be gone when no one might think to go look for her. But how could she accomplish that in the middle of the day with everyone so dutiful and concerned for her well-being? She was checked on and attended to almost constantly here. The minute she tried to disappear, someone would notice and raise the alarm.

If only she had an accomplice! Indeed, that would be perfect. But of course Braden's servants were loyal to him. No one here would help her to do anything to displease their master.

She kept her face passive and her voice even as Lord Braden led her back up to the ground floor. Something puzzled her. Had she really gotten that twisted around on their tour of the darkened passages, or did he lead her in a purposely non-direct route? Perhaps he was intentionally trying to get her confused.

Eventually, though, they made it back up to the warmer, brighter rooms of his living areas. It was quite a relief to be out of the damp. She shuddered to think of going back down there—alone. Or worse, *not* alone. And with chains.

"I hope you enjoyed your visit to my dungeon, Miss Horne," he said. "It is not the usual place to—"

They wer distracted by voices coming from inside the room they were passing. She recognized Mrs. Garver's voice, but had never heard the woman use this particular tone before. She sounded upset. Cassandra tried not to eavesdrop, but when her own name—or rather, Miss Horne's name—was mentioned, she could not help but pause in the doorway.

"I know you told me to put out the fire when Miss Horne left her room, but—" a young female voice was saying.

"But you let it burn," Mrs. Garver declared. "And now there's no coal for her and the wind blowing in through every crack in the walls."

"I'm sorry, ma'am. That's why I come down here to get more."

"Ye didn't find any, did you?" Mrs. Garver went on. "Now what's the poor lady to do, I ask ye? Cold as the devil today."

Lord Braden cleared his throat loudly. Mrs. Garver and a young maid glanced up and blinked in surprise to find them there, watching from the doorway. The maid dropped her gaze and gathered her apron into clenched fists. Mrs. Garver clenched her fists as well, but was far above aprons.

"Is there a problem?" Lord Braden asked.

"No sir," Mrs. Garver replied.

Lord Braden waited for explanation. He got none, so he went on.

"Did I hear you say there is no coal in Miss Horne's room right now?"

"I'm sorry, sir!" the maid said quickly, curtseying and blushing and wringing her apron. "I let it burn out."

Mrs. Garver frowned at her. "And on a day like today with the wind and the cold..."

"Indeed, this is not the weather to be without heat," Lord Braden said.

"I come here to get more," the girl offered quickly. "But I see that... er, I didn't find none. I'll just go to the coal bin below stairs—"

"No!"

Lord Braden's response was immediate and harsh. The girl jumped, and even Mrs. Garver's eyes went wide for a moment. Cassandra couldn't help but note she'd never heard him use that particular tone, either.

"No, not below stairs," he went on, more gently. "I'll see to it."

But Mrs. Garver was indignant. "The girl should correct her error, sir. I'll send her down."

"No, it is fine," he insisted. "She can tend other duties. I'll see to the coal for Miss Horne."

"I assure you it will be done right away, sir," Mrs. Garver said. "I'll go get a bucket myself."

"No! No, you needn't bother. I said I will get it."

His lordship's tone was so firm, so unarguable that Mrs. Garver and the maid simply exchanged worried looks but said nothing more. He dismissed them with final assurance that he alone would return to the lower level to fetch coal. The maid curtseyed and seemed happy to leave them. Mrs. Garver scowled after her.

"I am sorry for the oversight, my lord. It won't happen again."

"No worry, Mrs. Garver. The girl did not mean for the mistake. It will be remedied." he turned to Cassandra and smiled. "You will not go cold, my dear. I'll see to your coal."

"Er, thank you, sir."

Indeed, she had no doubt that he would. Mrs. Garver, however, seemed quite nonplussed by the unseemly notion that her master would stoop to so lowly a task. Cassandra, of course, knew what that was about. She had an inkling where this below-stairs coal room must be.

The dungeon area. Where his man was currently working. That was why Lord Braden had forbidden these servants to go there, insisting he be the one to gather more coal. He did not want them aware of what he was planning.

And why would he not want them to know? Because he feared what they might do. This was true insight she'd gained. So, Braden was not certain he could trust his servants with this knowledge. If they were truly loyal he would trust them, so what did this say? Obviously she'd been mistaken. Lord Braden could *not* rely on total cooperation from his staff. He knew not all of them would be in favor of something like kidnapping. Mrs. Garver would not be in favor of it.

This meant Cassandra had a glimmer of hope. This could be that accomplice, that ally she'd been missing. And as luck would have it, Lord Braden was eager to place her back into the older woman's keeping.

"Take Miss Horne up to her room now," he said, not nearly so eager for her company as he'd indicated while they were alone. "She's certainly due for a rest. Also, be sure to call for tea. That should warm her until I return with the coal for her grate."

"Of course, sir," Mrs. Garver agreed with a nod. "Come, Miss Horne. We'll have you feeling just the thing in no time."

She didn't bother to tell them she was already feeling just the thing. Hope had a way of doing that, she'd discovered.

He was rapidly losing hope that any of this would work out properly. Braden silently cursed everything from the cold air to Rovish's stubborness to Drake's poor timing as he marched back down the narrow, winding steps to the lower levels of the castle. He'd had Miss Horne there, wrapped in his arms and beaming up as she promised to be his wife. It had nearly made him forget the truth of his situation. He'd thought possibly everything would end well.

But then Drake barged in with his box of chain and the spell was broken. The look of terror on Miss Horne's face was a painful reminder that what he was doing should not be done, that he was acting less the dutiful husband and more the, well, lunatic. What could he be thinking, to steal from old Rovish and hope his staff and his bride might not find out? Foxes, of all things! They'd yelp and they'd smell and it would be just his luck they'd escape and find their way up to Miss Horne's chambers. How could he put a dozen silly foxes ahead of his duty to his home, his tenants, the woman he'd fallen in love with?

Yet, how could he not? Rovish's plan was cruel and appalling. If Braden had money he'd simply buy the man's mercy. But he had no money and Rovish had no mercy.

"Sorry about coming up on you when you had your lady down here," Drake said when Braden's footsteps alerted him to his returned presence.

"You were simply doing what you'd been told," Braden said briskly, hiding the spite that he felt. "I should never have brought Miss Horne down here."

"She seemed cozy enough. But why did you?"

"She asked and I simply could not refuse, I suppose."

"You're a ruined man, my lord."

"Don't I know it, Drake. I'm a fool if I think we can carry this out."

"So we're calling it off and Rovish will simply slaughter the poor beasties tomorrow?"

"No, of course we can't do that. Damn it, I should just step back and allow it, but I cannot."

"You've got a good heart, sir."

"I'm a fool, and you with me. What will Miss Horne say when she learns of this?"

"Why don't you tell her about it and find out what she'll say?"

"You're joking, right? You saw her expression. She'd been hoping to find something romantic down here; ancient treasure or swashbuckling tales. Instead, I showed her cobwebs, spiders, and a man who has nothing better to haul around than an old box of chain which, by the way, even I can't imagine what it's for."

"To shore up the wood rails I've got in place for keeping the foxes in that back cell you designated."

"You're not chaining the little things?"

"Of course not. The wood we used turned out to be rotted. Needs this chain wrapping it to keep it together. 'Specially since foxes chew."

"Oh. Very well, then. I just... We are doing the right thing, aren't we, Drake?"

"Of course, sir. And when your lady does find out about it—someday—she'll be very proud of you."

Braden was fairly sure that would not be the case. "Let's hope that she does not find out, shall we? She thinks me an honest man and I am determined to let her keep that illusion as long as possible."

Drake had the good sense to simply shrug his shoulders and tip an eyebrow, but he said nothing. Good man. Once the wedding was over and the weather improved enough for Braden to keep his promise and take his wife back to London where she could at last lay her father to rest and resume her life there, he would know he left MacMorton castle in capable hands.

"Illusions have a way of becoming *dis*illusions, my lord," Drake said.

He apparently chose not to elaborate, though, and Braden was happy enough for that. The last thing he needed was his steward waxing philosophical while they prepared to skulk out into the night and make off with his neighbor's illicit fox collection. What he *did* need was to be certain things here were set in perfect order to make their task as foolproof as possible. And to keep his mind off of Miss Horne.

Chapter 12

Mrs. Garver had been as accommodating as Cassandra could have possibly wished, but never once did she find opportunity to gain any hint that the woman might, after all, be the ally she needed to manage her unnoticed escape. Cassandra had gone so far as to be uncharacteristically demanding, in fact, eager to give the woman reason to grumble about her position here and open the door to productive conversation. When that failed, she'd tossed out little slights against Braden, hoping the housekeeper might subtly agree. It was all to no avail.

"Ah, here's the girl with your tea, Miss," the housekeeper said.

Somehow she kept her voice cheerful even after Cassandra had made her set her up in the bed, then asked to be moved to a chair, then been tucked into yet another chair and supplied with one blanket after another. The woman never complained and Cassandra ended up swaddled and swathed as if she were an incapable infant.

Tea was set out and a steaming cup placed in her hands as per Lord Braden's order. Mrs. Garver hovered nearby and recited over and over that his lordship would soon arrive with the coal, as if at any moment some grave infection might fall upon Cassandra simply because there was no fire in the grate. Clearly it would be quite risky to trust this woman with her plans, yet she had little other hope. She would try once more to gain support for plans to leave.

"I was amazed in my tour of the castle today," she said between sips.

"MacMorton is an amazing place," Mrs. Garver agreed.

"I couldn't help but wonder how the staff can keep up with it all. It appears quite vast, and I saw only a handful of servants."

"We do our work, Miss," the housekeeper said and seemed insulted she should suggest otherwise. "Everyone here is quite competent, I assure you."

"Oh, I have no doubt. I simply wondered that Lord Braden does not maintain a larger staff. I would hate to think any of you are overworked."

But even that would not tempt the woman into betraying her master.

"His lordship is more than fair with us. Not a soul in the castle feels he or she is uncared for or disrespected. It is an honor to serve a man such as Lord Braden."

Drat. Mrs. Garver seemed to have nothing but praise for the man. But Cassandra was not giving up. There must be something she could say that would open the door to making a friend—a friend who would agree to helping her escape.

"Er, I am happy to hear that. As you can imagine, I have been more than a bit concerned for his character."

"Concerned, Miss? Lord Braden is of the finest character. You have no cause for concern."

"I'm sure he appears so, but truly, you cannot be

unaware of the situation around you. You must have noticed some things are not quite as they should be... not as a dutiful master should keep them."

The woman's chin rose defiantly. "And what things might these be, Miss Horne?"

"The carpets, for one. Oh, I'm not saying they aren't quite clean, but hasn't his lordship noticed their condition? And... and there are places where the roof actually sags! Surely he cannot ignore that in good conscience."

"There is nothing at all wrong with Lord Braden's conscience."

"Perhaps not. Still... I worry that if a man can allow his home to be so neglected, how must he treat the people under his care?"

Unfortunately, this was enough to give offense. It seemed Cassandra's efforts had produced the opposite of what she'd been attempting. Instead of seeing a kindred soul, Mrs. Garver was now ready to go to war.

"Lord Braden is the finest man imaginable. He would do *anything* for the well-being of his home and the people under his care. It's shameful how his father left things. Now poor Braden has nothing left but to shackle himself for life with a..."

"Yes?"

"Forgive me, miss. I am out of line. His lordship would not have me speak this way, so I won't. If there is anything else that you need, then—"

Lord Braden appeared in her doorway.

"Er, sorry to take so long with this."

He entered, carrying a scuttle of coal, and went directly to her grate. If he'd overheard any of their conversation he gave no indication. Mrs. Garver flitted about nervously, handing him the tinderbox and looking as guilty as if she'd stolen from him.

Cassandra had to avert her eyes from him as he crouched over the fire. Her teacup was not nearly so interesting as the man's form while he labored to position the coal and strike the tinder, but she refused to admire anything other than the tiny rosebuds that circled her saucer. She could not help but be aware of him, though, and wonder what he must think if he had overheard her impugning his skill as lord and master of MacMorton.

"Thank you, my lord," she said when he had the fire going and the first traces of warmth touched her.

He rose to full height and smiled at her. She was determined not to let herself fall prey again to those deep, searching gazes and the tempting thrill of his nearness. It was nearly impossible to reconcile this man before her to the man she had heard plotting against her. Yet then again, she'd seen the condition of his home. If, as Mrs. Garver seemed to indicate, this was not due to some failing on his part, then the only other explanation was that he simply did not have the means to make things better.

And a man with no means could easily become desperate. Indeed, she had only her own father to look at for proof. Afterall, hadn't Mrs. Garver said he would do anything for the well-being of his home? Apparently the man had ample motivation to cast in his lot with Mr. Rovish and be prepared to resort to abduction.

Still... his smile was so warm, his expression sincere.

"I hope you are quite comfortable, my dear," he said, leaving the grate to come to her side.

He crouched down again, but this time it was not a fire in the grate he was igniting. Ah, but those eyes... she swallowed back her girlish reactions and nodded politely.

"I am, sir. Thank you. Mrs. Garver has been most attentive."

"I am glad. You know I would never want for you to be unhappy here."

"Er, thank you."

She was rapidly losing her battle to remain immune to the man. She was forgetting even why she should remain immune. He had the most enchanting creases at the corners of his expressive eyes...

"You are pale," he said and she wondered how he could possibly think so, as heated as her cheeks were. "You should rest now."

At that he rose again and it was all she could do to keep from clutching at his arm to keep him near. Heavens, what a ninny she was becoming. The sooner he took his leave from her the better.

"Mrs. Garver, I thank you for seeing to her so diligently. This should be more than enough coal to keep the room warm now. I suggest we allow Miss Horne to finish her tea then retire for a time. I have hope that the physician will soon be located and we can all be assured of her continued recovery, but in the meanwhile I insist that we provide a restful atmosphere."

"Of couse," Mrs. Garver said. "I will see that Miss Horne is undisturbed until it is time to dress for dinner."

He frowned. "Oh. Yes, dinner. Er, I'm afaid I won't be dining tonight. Likely Miss Horne would be best to simply remain where she's comfortable. You'll see that she is brought a tray, won't you?"

Mrs. Garver seemed as confused and surprised by this as Cassandra. The man wasn't dining? What gentleman did not dine? It could only mean he had other plans—and she had a fair idea what those might be. How convenient for him to instruct his servants to leave her alone and unattended for the evening, alone with just a tray. He could do as he liked with her then, couldn't he? She shuddered.

It was not altogether an unpleasant shudder, though. It was entirely a new sort of shudder. *That* realization made her shudder again.

He hated to leave her. She seemed so vulnerable and alone, all bundled up like a child in a blanket, sipping her tea and trying not to look at him. But she was not a child. It was impossible for him not to be very much aware of that every moment he was near her.

Mrs. Garver assured him she would be looked after, but that her rest would be uninterrupted. He could only hope that would be the case. He prayed she would sleep soundly, perfectly oblivious to his foolhardy actions while her bruises mended and her strength returned. Then tomorrow his deeds would be done, she would wake and would become his wife.

A thrill of anxious expectation ran through him. *His wife.* The reality of it still could not quite sink in. He would be a married man, and he was actually quite pleased at the thought of it.

For now, though, he could not think of it. He needed to keep his wits about him. He would meet Drake and tend to the last of their preparations, talk through their plans and make certain every detail was in place. Drake had recruited several of the stable hands to assist, although Braden would have preferred not to involve any innocent parties. He hated to think that his servants would risk involvement in such underhanded activities for his sake, but it seemed they were only too happy to involve themselves in anything that caused aggravation for the unpleasant Rovish.

Since Braden could completely understand that feeling, and due to the fact that extra hands were fully needed for this task, he gave in and allowed for their plan to incorporate them. By the time tonight's strategy was in place, every man knew his job and eager to go. They took on this burden as if it were their own and Braden was half convinced he himself was not even needed. But he would go, by God. This was his project. He would face the consequences should things go badly. It was his duty to see that they did not.

Drake had prepared a wagon, specially fitted with a large box hidden under what appeared to be a mound of hay. The hope was that they might arrive undetected at the shed behind the rustic hunting box where he had been secretly—so he thought—housing the foxes. The old fool knew Braden never used the place, even though it was on MacMorton lands. Previous Braden's had used the hunting box, hosting parties to hunt and carouse, but the cottage had sat empty for years now.

If Braden were not such a lover of nature and had made it a practice to travel his lands to observe them, he never would have noticed the unauthorized traps Rovish had scattered about. He alerted his steward who set men out to watch. They'd discovered what Rovish was up to, but because Braden's damnable father had mortgaged the lands and given rights for their usage to old Rovish for life, Braden had no legal right to stop it.

He would stop it, though. The men he'd sent to spy on old Rovish said the foxes were generally left alone, penned up in crates in that shed. Apparently Rovish had not required any of his servants to stay out there and tend to them; he merely sent boys once a day to toss the poor creatures some chicken carcasses and other scraps from Rovish's kitchens. Braden could not be sure what condition they'd find the animals in by the time they got there.

Their plan was to move in quickly while no one was around, scoop up the foxes one at a time and put them in sturdy bags. Carefully, of course. The bags would keep them calm, actually, and make it unlikely they might hurt themselves from fear. Each bag would be placed into the box on the wagon and the hay would—theoretically, at least—muffle the sounds that a dozen freshly bagged foxes might make.

In this weather there should be no one out in the forest to see them or hear them, but Braden felt they could not be too careful. Everything would be handled as quickly and silently as possible after the sun had gone down. Once back at MacMorton, the creatures would be gently released from confinement into the roomy area that had been designated safe for them in the dungeon.

Hopefully it would not be long before Braden could make the necessary reparations to Rovish so that a feud did not erupt over this. Surely Rovish would not want the scandal that should come if people were to find that he espoused such suspect hunting practices and was trespassing so freely on Braden's property. He would accept Braden's payment and at that point the animals would not need to be hidden. Braden could move them to an outdoor area that might be better suited for retraining them to live in the wild.

At least, that was the plan. It was just after dark now, so very soon they would see how it played out. He and Drake were just leaving his office to go meet the others when Mrs. Garver came scurrying in.

"He's here, my lord," she said in a hurried, breathless voice.

"He? He who?"

"The physician! The one you called for; the one up from London."

Well, this was a surprise, but not objectionable. He would have preferred to leave Miss Horne undisturbed, but getting her medical attention was certainly of highest priority. He'd have Mrs. Garver take the man up to see her immediately.

"So my rider was able to locate him," he said. "Excellent. See that he has everything he needs, Mrs. Garver, and take him up to Miss Horne."

She did not seem content with his response. "Er, he insists on speaking with you first, my lord."

"He does?"

Probably to make certain he'd get his payment. Braden couldn't actually blame the man, considering what he may have heard about things at the estate. Still, the timing was bad and Braden simply could not afford a delay.

"I must tend to something, Mrs. Gaver, but assure him I'll see him as soon as I can."

"He's very adamant, sir. He says it's quite urgent."

Damn. More urgent than tending to Miss Horne?

This was not the sort of thing Braden needed just now. He glanced over at Drake, who shrugged.

"You should see him, my lord. I'll go look after our business."

"What? Without me?"

Drake frowned. "You doubt we can handle it?"

"Of course not. But it is my responsibility."

"If you don't mind me saying, sir, the young lady is your responsibility."

"Yes, she is but..."

"I've got the boys and everything's ready. We'll take care of it. You go take care of your bride."

It seemed such a foreign concept, but Braden was at a loss to find reason to argue. Besides, Mrs. Garver was watching him like a hawk. A very worried hawk with a strange physician in her entry hall.

"Very well," he said finally. "Go, Drake, but take care. I will meet this physician and look after Miss Horne. Don't let us require anything further from the good doctor tonight."

"No worries," Drake assured him.

He made no further argument. And why should he? Drake knew what would happen if something occurred to keep Braden from marrying the heiress. Their only hope of pacifying Rovish once this was done—and avoidance of possible prosecution—was the money this marriage would bring into the estate.

As for Braden, he had to admit he would rest easier knowing Miss Horne was quite well. The foxes would just have to be entrusted to others tonight. He clapped Drake on the back and sent him on his way with cryptic words of encouragement. Mrs. Garver was still in the dark about their plan and he preferred to keep it that way. When Drake was away he gave himself to her.

"Now I am free for the doctor. Please send him in, Mrs. Garver."

He went back to his desk and had not yet settled into his chair when the housekeeper returned. She still appeared nervous, but this time she brought with her a winded looking middle-aged man, still damp from the elements.

"Dr. Morrow," she introduced.

The man bustled past her and into the office.

"What's this I hear about James Horne being dead?"

Braden had risen to his feet to greet the man and was glad for it. The physician's demeanor was anything but caring and concerned.

"I'm sorry, sir," Braden said with a coolness he did not feel. "You are acquainted with the man?"

"I just left him three days ago, in Birmingham."

"I'm sorry, but he's no longer there."

"I don't see how he could not be, if I left him there. Alive, I might add."

"He and his daughter were traveling here," Braden explained. "The roads are quite bad, you may have noticed."

"Of course I noticed. That's why I left them in Birmingham and continued this way without them."

"Continued this way?"

"Your man found me in Derby. I've no clue how Horne could have passed me and then met his end, all in but three days time."

"Unfortunately, he did. Miss Horne, I'm happy to say, appears well, although I would be ever grateful if you could examine her and assure me of that. She suffered some bruising and quite a shock in the accident, as you can imagine."

He didn't pause to imagine. "The shock is finding them here when I believe them to be elsewhere."

"Perhaps they *were* in Birmingham, sir, but I assure you, they are in MacMorton now. Well, Miss Horne is, at least. Her father and coachman, I'm sorry to say, are temporary residents of my ice house."

"The coachman?"

"Yes. He, too, was killed in the accident."

"And Miss Horne... she is not overcome?"

"She was injured, but she seems to be recovering."

"But... she is aware of the deaths of her father and her... er, the coachman?"

"Yes, she asked to see her father this morning, but she was fully composed. Quite a remarkable woman, as a matter of fact."

"Composed? Indeed, that is remarkable. I've never known Miss Horne to... and you say she has suffered no ill effects from the accident?"

"Bruises, of course, and she was somewhat confused right at first, but she has rebounded quite well. At least, she gives every indication. I am hoping that you can confirm her good health mostly for my own peace of mind. We are planning to be wed, you must know."

It appeared the good doctor did not know this at all. He seemed quite surprised. "Wed? But I... that is, when I left them..."

"Did they not mention? She and I have corresponded for months now. I had some business with her father and he suggested we might be well suited and... well, they were traveling here so that we might be wed. Just how well *did* you know the family,

Dr. Morrow?"

"Very well, so I thought. I tended her mother through the last years of her life, and have been physician to Miss Horne ever since. It was I who... but she has agreed to marry you, sir?"

"She has, and seems quite happy for it. Really now, doctor, shouldn't you be asking to see the patient by now and not rattle on with these questions that have no reason?"

"Oh, I have reason, my lord. I assure you. Reason you might want to hear, as a matter of fact."

"And what could that be?"

"Quite simply, Miss Horne is a liar."

Chapter 13

To be honest, Cassandra had expected her escape from MacMorton castle to be far more difficult. As it was, she found all she needed to do was open her door, peer out into the corridor, then head for the servants' stair she'd found on the previous night. Mrs. Garver had left a lantern for her and she'd layered herself with clothing and her coat, then draped the two shawls she'd been given over it all.

Things appeared to be working out far better than anticipated. She only took two wrong turns before she finally found her way to the kitchens. This would be the trickiest part of her escape—no doubt there was a full complement of servants in this area. But, the only passage she knew that led down into the lower levels of the castle was near here. She'd used the kitchens as her reference when memorizing the layout during her tour earlier. She would simply have to make it through this part of the house without drawing any attention to herself.

This, it turned out, was not as easy as she'd hoped. Oh, none of Lord Braden's servants happened to notice her as she moved past the kitchens, darting from shadow to shadow in the corridors between rooms, but one of her newest friends did. The kitten.

It appeared at her heel, mewing and batting at the corners of the shawls as they dragged along behind her. How she had attracted the little darling she had no idea, but even when she hoisted up the tantalizing shawls and tried to shoo it away, it still followed. This was not helpful.

Since she could not have the mewing or the patter of pouncing kitten paws give her away, she stooped down to pick up the little feline. It purred and pressed its head into her palm. She smiled.

Perhaps no one would notice if he came along with her. Certainly he was too small to cause any trouble for her, and she could easily hide him under her shawl if needed. It might be nice to have some company on her journey home, actually. Lord Braden would never miss him and she... well, she would always cherish the fluffy reminder of her very brief time here.

She snuggled him and moved silently along toward the stone arch at the end of the corridor. It was dark and foreboding, but she knew once she was on her way down that ancient staircase—away from the kitchens and Braden's staff—she could unshutter her lantern and relax just a bit. Then it was a simple matter of finding her way to that door she had pointed out earlier. That door would be her exit.

After that, she would simply have to hope she could find her way to the village she'd heard mentioned. The servants had spoken of it being downstream, so at least she knew what direction to go. It must be in walking distance, else how could they travel back and forth? She would find it.

Once there, she could use Papa's money to buy passage. On someting. Surely someone would gladly trade transport for coin. She'd make her way to some town—any town, really—then take the mail coach back to Grandmother. It seemed very practical as she thought it all through. She could only hope it would go as planned in actual practice.

The sounds and smells from the kitchens faded behind her as she made her way down the passage. Her boots clacked on the cold stone steps, so she moved carefully, holding the lantern in front of her and reciting over and other that she had nothing to fear. No one knew she was here, so no one would be looking for her. She had simply to keep placing one foot in front of the other.

The passage curved to the right, the stair taking her deeper and deeper below the castle. She reached the point where she could not see the top of the steps behind her, nor the bottom in front. The purring kitten in her arms was an enormous source of comfort. As if this tiny thing could offer her any real protection. Still, it was nice not being alone.

It would have been even nicer to have been with Lord Braden again. She'd felt very secure as she traveled this route with him earlier. But of course, he was the one she was escaping. She should be glad he was not here.

She should be, but she wasn't.

At last she reached the bottom of the stairs. She had to pause there, remembering which way to turn next. Had they gone right, or had they gone left? She'd tried to pay attention, but it was such a huge dungeon, with so many passages branching out in all directions.

Left, she decided. She turned and followed the flickering pool of light from her lantern. Cobwebs dangled in every corner and she refused to think of what other small creatures might be eyeing her progress. There was nothing that could hurt her. She'd be out of this place soon.

But "soon" gradually became "at some point" and, after retracing her steps for the third time in hopes of finding a familiar passage, it became "eventually". And even that was more wishful than certain. The cold and damp had sunk into her bones and she was forced to admit she was lost. The kitten had fallen asleep, but she was wide awake and her heart pounded as she found herself in yet another unrecognizable area of this horrible dungeon.

Where was that door? How was she to get out of here? Heavens, she could not even find her way back up into the castle at this point. The last thing she wanted was to be trapped down here all night! Perhaps this had been a foolish plan, after all.

Then, as she stood there feeling silly and wondering what to do, she felt a breeze. Just the slightest brush of cool air—but air that was moving. It smelled like outdoors—fresh with a hint of the earth and of pine. This was all very welcome at this point.

She held up her lantern and hurried forward, following this breeze. Yes, she could feel the air getting colder and fresher. She was getting nearer to...

Here it was, the dim but wide corridor that she recalled from earlier! Thank heavens. The small passage she was in opened into a larger one, a main one. Somehow she'd gotten lost from it, but now here it was. Lord Braden had taken her along this main passage, she was certain.

She turned toward the breeze and her lantern

flickered, lighting up the area around her. Casks. Yes, these were the broken casks he said had once been used for the castle's ale. Then the door to the outside should be... indeed, there it was. Just as she recalled. But this time it was open!

This was the source of that air she'd been feeling. How very odd! The man had said no one used this door. She'd expected it to be closed, had worried even that she might have trouble opening it on her own. But here it stood wide open, the chill of night air drafting down the stone steps on the other side and bringing outdoor scents into this dungeon. But who could be using the door?

"How good to find you here, Miss Loring."

A voice in the darkness behind her, near the casks. She knew that voice! Good heavens, it was Mr. Rovish. But wasn't he dead? Apparently not.

He came into view, his filthy clothes all askew and his face swollen and bruised. Was his nose bent at an odd angle, too? She believed that it was. He looked even more evil and menacing than she recalled him.

She shuddered and backed away, but he stepped out from the shadows and came toward her. He moved with a limp, his hand clutching a stout stick as if for a cane. Or a weapon.

'You're looking well, Miss Loring," he said.

"I... er, thank you. And you..."

She really could not finish that statement. It would have been polite to return his compliment, but of course he did not look well and she could certainly not say it was good to see him again. Truly, she could think of nothing polite to say to the man, considering the circumstance. She wanted to dash out the doorway and up those cold steps.

But he jumped in front of her, blocking her way and raising his stick to remind her that he was not a nice man.

"Thinking of leaving?" he asked. "Why? What is Braden doing, plotting and scheming down here?"

Of course she *had* been thinking of leaving, and Braden *was* plotting and scheming in his dungeon, but she felt no compulsion to tell this man anything about it. Especially if he did not already know.

"No. Nothing. I was exploring the castle and found myself down here. That's all."

"So you are in it with him, are you? I should have known he'd win you over, the moony-eyed sap. What's he up to? What's he planning to do to my father?"

"Lord Braden is not a moony-eyed... wait, planning to do to your father?"

"He's been harassing my father for years, ever since the old Lord Braden hung up his spoon and everyone learned he had mortgaged half his estate to my father."

"Your father holds a mortgage on MacMorton Castle?"

"No, not the bloody castle, thank God. Just the land. Some of it—what's not entailed. But Braden isn't satisfied with what he inherited outright. He wants it all back unencumbered. Seems the earl hasn't been happy with the terms—we get to hunt for his game and do whatever we like on his precious Braden land as long as Father still holds that mortgage."

"So, he conspires with you in order to pay off the mortgage?"

Mr. Rovish snorted and shifted his weight with a grimace. "Pay it off? Oh, he's tried. But my father rather likes Braden's land. We've made it nearly impossible for your dear earl to pay what he owes. My father plans to keep things that way for a good long time."

"I see."

Indeed, she did not. What was she to make of this new information? Mr. Rovish was actually from this area—no wonder he had brought her here to conduct his dirty dealings. His father was Braden's neighbor and Braden was beholden to him. This could explain why Braden was working with him. Yet Mr. Rovish seemed just as perplexed by what Braden was doing down here as she. Could it be he was not in league with the man? Then what was Braden up to?

"So tell me," Mr. Rovish continued, inching closer to her. "How has Lord Braden sucked you into this feud? How is he planning to use you in all this?"

He seemed truly convinced that whatever Lord Braden was plotting involved his family, not Cassandra's abduction. She supposed this must be good news. But she'd over heard the man plotting, and he'd clearly talked of keeping someone captive down here. Could it possibly be he had not been referring to her? Then who on earth was Lord Braden planning to kidnap?

She was more confused than ever now. Things were all fuzzy in her brain; so much had happened and her mind was a jumble. She frowned.

"I don't know what you are talking about," she said finally. "Now if you please, I wish to leave."

"Oh, no you don't." He brought up his cane, backing her into the wall. "Tell me what he's up to. What's Braden about, sending men to spy on my father and poke around at the hunting box?"

"Hunting box? What hunting box?"

"My father's hunting box! Well, I suppose it's actually Braden's, but since he's all lily-livered and refuses to hunt like a gentleman, my father is the one left to use it."

"Your father uses Lord Braden's hunting box? I can't imagine the earl takes very kindly to that."

Indeed, she could not imagine it. Lord Braden gave safe harbor to badgers, filled his home with all manner of creatures, wild and tame. She could quite well imagine he did not take kindly to any of the Rovishs killing his game or making use of his buildings. Yes, more and more she was beginning to believe whatever Lord Braden was scheming just might have more to do with Mr. Rovish than her.

Well, that was a fine thing to learn now that she was already here in the dungeon, far from anyone friendly, and faced with a half-crazed murderer.

"I wonder if Braden will take kindly to you wandering off this way?" Mr. Rovish said with that awful leer she'd come to despise.

"He has told me to make myself at home in his castle," she replied.

The tension in the air was almost as strong as the chill. The kitten woke and she rubbed its tiny ear to help calm it. Or perhaps more to calm herself. The kitten did not quite seem to comprehend the menace in their situation.

"Make yourself at home, eh?" Rovish grinned. It was not a pleasant sight. One tooth was cracked and jagged. "I see. So his lordship knows a good thing when he finds one. Has he already lured you into his bed, or has he nobly offered you marriage first?"

"How dare you!"

"I see. So he's left you alone, then. The man *is* a lily-livered fool. But I suppose he's gotten you to agree to marry him, eh? Yes, your eyes tell me I'm correct."

He laughed at her. An ugly sound, and bits of spittle sprinkled her skin. She held the kitten tighter, safely under her shawl.

"It's none of your business. Now move aside. I wish to go."

"Such airs! It's as if you think you're already the countess here. I imagine you will be soon enough, though. No doubt Braden has insisted on a hasty wedding?"

"You've no idea what you're talking about."

"Oh, but don't tell me... the man has made you fall in love with him! Well, this is rich. Here I was, thinking you had more of a brain than that. You can't possibly believe he might honestly care for you?"

He was deplorable and she was getting angry. "Of course I have more brain than that. Lord Braden doesn't even know who—" She stopped herself short.

"What? *What* doesn't he know?"

"I will not speak to you. Get out of my way, Mr. Rovish."

But he didn't. He moved even closer, his stick held just high enough that he could swing it at her in an instant. She'd been completely an idiot to let herself get into this position.

"There *is* something going on here, isn't there, Miss Loring? Braden is up to something and you know about it. Now tell me!"

"No! Leave me alone. He will find you here and he'll... he'll kill you."

She had tried to sound confident and threatening, but apparently she'd merely been pitiful. Mr. Rovish laughed at her.

"Kill me? Lord Braden? He hasn't the stomach for it, Miss Loring. He's not man enough to kill a rabbit, let alone defend trash like you."

"He's twice the man you are, Mr. Rovish."

"Oh? Allow me to prove you wrong, pretty dove."

"You disgust me."

"I don't doubt it. But if you want to live, you'll do exactly as I say."

"I won't do anything you say."

"You'll do *everything* I say."

He grabbed for her. She jerked and tried to pull away, but his fist latched around the layers of shawls. In her struggle to escape the shawls were ripped away and he flailed at her arms. The kitten was dislodged and tumbled to the floor, screeching and scrambling for a place to hide in the sudden tumult.

Mr. Rovish was startled and raised his stick to attack whatever this terrified ball of fur might be. Cassandra cried out and grabbed his arm.

"Don't hurt it! It's only a kitten!"

He paused, the lantern swinging wildly in her hand but enough light flicking over the tiny creature to confirm her words. Rovish laughed and bent to snatch it up. She moved toward him to rescue it, but his big hand clamped over its tiny head. The muffled mews almost broke her heart.

"Do as I say, Miss Loring, or I crush this useless animal right in front of you."

"No! Put it down, please."

"When you are being more agreeable, perhaps I

will. Now, set aside that annoying lantern and—"

But his words were broken off as a barrage of muffled shouts and clattering feet sounded at the top of the darkened steps leading up from the open doorway near them. Someone was coming down! A great number of someones, from the sound of it. She would be saved!

"Make a peep and the cat is dead," Mr. Rovish hissed. "Keep quiet and come."

He grabbed her arm with one hand but kept the other firmly over the kitten's head. The poor little thing swung in the air, kicking as best it could but having little effect over the horrible man. Cassandra sucked in her breath and worried at any moment the tiny creature might go limp and be done for. She didn't dare argue with Mr. Rovish and was forced to let him drag her off into the darkness.

He pulled her away from the store of rotted casks and down another passage—the same one where she'd seen Lord Braden's man carrying his crate full of chains. Was that man, perhaps unknown to Lord Braden, partnered with Mr. Rovish? She hated to think it.

And just who was the noisy group heading toward them? By Rovish's reaction she could gather they were not friends of his. Then again, that would not necessarily make them friends of hers, either. And she had no way to alert them to her situation if she did not want Rovish to instantly wring the poor kitten's neck.

The brute dragged her around a corner and her lantern light fell across what could only be described as a cage. One apparent cell in a dark nook was boarded up with planks then strewn over with chain. The door to the cell stood open and Rovish chuckled grimly as he shoved her inside.

"This looks perfect," he said. "We'll just wait here until things settle down. Douse the light. Oh, please be as loud as you like, if you enjoy seeing little things suffer."

As she did not like seeing little things suffer, she did as he said. The light in the cell went dim. In the back of her mind she ran through her available options. She could not count on anyone to find her here, no one knew she was gone. The men clambering down the stone steps were likely delivering coal or some other commodity and would not come back this way. Her predicament seemed dismal. At least the kitten still mewed. She prayed it suffered no permanent damage from the deplorable treatment.

"Into the corner," Rovish growled. "And keep silent."

Why hadn't she thought to take some sort of weapon with her when she left the warm security of her room upstairs? This botched escape was becoming more and more regrettable with every heartbeat. She should never have left. She should have simply confessed the truth to Lord Braden and trusted him, begged him for mercy. Even if he had been plotting with Rovish—as unlikely as that seemed to her now—she could not bring herself to believe that man on his worst day could come close to the things Mr. Rovish was capable of.

Now she'd put herself and an innocent kitten in peril. She glanced around the dim cell, desperate for her eyes to catch on anything that might be used against her captor. She saw nothing. It was as if the place has been scoured clean, made safe enough for children to play.

There was nothing but a few fresh mats laid out here and there, as if for someone small to curl up and take a pleasant nap. What a strange place!

The sounds of approaching footsteps and hushed voices got louder. And something else, too. Along with the decidedly human sounds there were other noises; odd yelps and squeals. What on earth could be making such commotion? And were her ears deceiving her, or were the sounds coming directly their way?

Mr. Rovish grumbled another warning in her ear and tugged her close up against him, pressing them both into the deepest, darkest corner of the cell. The voices were just outside now, then the chains rattled as something banged against them. The yelping continued.

All had been dark, with just the tiniest sliver of light coming from her shuttered lantern, but now more faint flickers could be seen through the wooden planks at the front of their cell. Whoever was coming carried light with them. Oh, please God, let them look into the cell and notice her! And then let them not turn out to be even worse scoundrels than Mr. Rovish.

"What do you know of Miss Horne," Braden asked the physician, already prepared to argue with the man whatever his answer might be.

"She never had any intention of marrying you," the doctor said. "I'm sorry, sir, but it was all her father's doing. He was the one who wanted the match."

"Miss Horne has been very honest in her expectations, sir. I understand that she was hesitant at first, and made many demands as to the conditions of our union, but now that she is here... well, our arrangement has become much more of an agreement."

"Has it, now? You are certain she wishes to marry you?"

"Of course. I have heard it from her own lips."

"And did she tell you she was breeding?"

This stopped any line of discourse Braden was mentally preparing. What was this man inferring? Miss Horne was... in a delicate way? No, he could not believe it.

"That cannot be true."

"It *is* true. I am her physician and I know it to be very true."

"But what... who..?"

"The coachman. He was far more that just her father's servant to her. Miss Horne had intentions of running off to marry him; it was her father's wish that she do far better and marry a gentleman."

"But that cannot be," Braden said, rapidly turning pages in his memory of every conversation he'd had with Miss Horne. "She never showed any sign of grief for the man, nothing that would signify..."

Then again, she had asked after the coachman, hadn't she? Indeed, right at first. She seemed concerned about the condition he'd been found in... yes, but at the time it had seemed nothing more than the usual compassion one might show in such situation. Could the woman have really been hiding her emotion so well? She'd not shed a tear, asked only to be shown her father's body. Indeed, the physician's assertion made no sense at all.

"Miss Horne and her father's coachman had been hiding an affair for some time," the older man explained. "The only reason she agreed to this journey was because it seemed an excellent opportunity for her and her lover to escape farther north, to Gretna Green. I'm afraid I am the one who foiled their plan, actually, by insisting that her father know what was going on."

"You told Mr. Horne?"

"I did."

"And, er, how did he receive the news?"

"Furious at first, of course, but he cares deeply for his daughter and came to realize that her happiness was more important to him than gaining a title in the family. He agreed to allow their marriage and that is why they stayed in Birmingham and did not continue the journey. Mr. Horne sent me on to relay the message to you, thinking it might give less offense delivered in person rather than by note."

"Less offense? I agree, I am not offended, merely confused."

"As am I," the physician confessed. "I simply cannot imagine how it could be they arrived here before me, or what may have changed Mr. Horne's mind."

"And we certainly cannot go ask him. I suppose Miss Horne, herself, is the only one who can answer."

"Indeed, sir. She owes you that, at least, I would say."

"Very well. We will go talk to Miss Horne."

Mrs. Garver suddenly appeared in the doorway. "But you cannot, sir!"

"I beg your pardon?" Braden asked.

"She's gone, my lord!"

Mrs. Garver's face was pale and her expression gave him no doubt she was telling the truth. Not that her words made any more sense than the doctor's had. Miss Horne was with child by her dead coachman and now she was *gone*? It was all ludicrous.

"How can she be gone?" Braden asked.

"I don't know. I left ye to go check on her and found her room empty."

"Did you look... is she, perhaps, indisposed?"

"I've looked everywhere, my lord! There's no sign of her, and... her clothes are all gone, too. Wherever she is, she dressed warmly."

Braden frowned. What the devil could the girl be up to? Where could she go? And then it dawned on him.

"The ice house! She may have gone there to grieve over the bodies again."

"Yes, that would make sense," the physician said. "Though I don't know that it could be very good for her."

"No, she should not be alone. It is well after dark now."

He was already on the way to collect a lantern. The doctor followed, with Mrs. Garver fluttering behind them, uttering oaths of regret for managing to lose track of the girl and worrying for her well-being. Braden would hate to see the woman's reaction when she learned the full truth of Miss Horne.

Indeed, he was uncertain of his own reaction to it. Miss Horne had agreed to marry him, knowing full well that she carried another man's child. Of course, she was hardly in a position to refuse him, at this point. Her father and her lover both lay dead, what choice did the girl have but to accept him? And what choice did he have but to go through with it?

Yes, he was having quite a reaction to that. He did not like it at all. He still wanted to rush out to that ice house and sweep Miss Horne into his arms, oddly enough, but now he also wanted and grab up the dead coachman and strangle him. Never mind that the man's neck was already broken and his corpse a blood-covered mess.

He threw on warm clothes and a footman quickly produced the good doctor's damp cloak. They were out into the darkness in no time and rushing along the muddy path toward the ice house. The physician seemed as eager to find the girl as Braden was.

As they approached, though, it appeared their guess had been wrong. The great door to the cave carved into the hill was still closed. Braden had to yank it quite hard to pull it open and no light shone inside. They stepped in.

There was no sign of Miss Horne. Everything was as they had left it. Blocks of ice carved from nearby lakes during winter sat on pallets of wood, the floor covered in sawdust with bags of the stuff propped here and there to help preserve the ice. Stretched out on the ice were the bodies, just as they had been. Mr. Horne's shroud showed signs of having been shifted a bit, but the coachman seemed exactly as he had been when Braden oversaw their placement here two full days ago. Miss Horne had mourned over her father, but she'd apparently not touched her lover's broken body. That seemed odd, for some reason.

"She isn't here," the doctor noted.

"No. I brought her here earlier, but she only asked to visit her father's body. See her footprints in the sawdust? There is no indication she went near the other man."

"This is Mr. Horne?"

"Yes, this one."

"He was badly damaged in the accident, then?"

"No, he had barely a scratch," Braden said, perplexed by the physician's curiosity and the way he gazed at the shrouded form. "Why do you ask?"

"Mr. Horne is a very large man, sir. This body, oddly enough, appears to be of a quite slight man."

"This is her father, sir. She confirmed it herself."

The physician made no comment, but went to the body and pulled back the shroud. The pale face of Mr. Horne was there, just as Braden had last seen it, if perhaps a bit paler and more sunken in appearance.

Finally the physician turned to him and spoke.

"This not James Horne."

"What? Of course it is. Who else could it be?"

"I have no idea, my lord, but this man is not Mr. Horne."

"But how could she be so mistaken? Surely a girl knows her own father?"

"Unless the girl is not Miss Horne."

Not Miss Horne? It was unthinkable. Who else could she be? Of course she was Miss Horne! She had never suggested otherwise. She had... well, she had been confused about some aspects of their past correspondence, hadn't she? And come to think of it, hadn't she been surprised by her own name when he'd used it?

Of course, everything fit. No wonder the woman he'd come to know these past days had been nothing like the person who'd written him letters. He should have known there was no way someone could present herself so differently. His Miss Horne was not really Miss Horne.

"So who have I been harboring in my house for

three days?" Braden mused aloud.

Bloody hell. Who was the girl, and what did all this mean? Well, for one it likely meant she wasn't pregnant with some coachman's ruddy bastard, whoever she was. But to think, he'd proposed marriage to her! Still rather fancied himself in love, as a matter of fact. Could he honestly still care for her, knowing she was a liar? Only a fool would do that. All he knew for certain was that his mystery girl was missing and, by God, he was going to find her.

"She must be a thief," the physician said. "She insinuated herself into your house, likely to steal from you."

If that were the case, the girl left no doubt very disappointed. No one had fewer valuables worth stealing than Lord Braden, these days. Besides, there would have been much, much easier ways to get into his home to steal.

"That carriage accident was quite violent," Braden said. "I can't imagine it was staged intentionally. Perhaps... perhaps she suffered some injury that allowed her to forget her identity. When she awoke she simply accepted that she was Miss Horne because we all called her that."

"I suppose that could be possible," the doctor allowed. "Still, it would seem unlikely she gave you no indication of this. Patients with extreme brain confusion generally suffer other symptoms, or come down with fever."

"Perhaps she has," Braden said, a panic taking over his insides. "Perhaps that's why she's gone missing. She could be out of her mind, endangering herself, even."

"Quite possible." They physician nodded,

contemplating this notion. "Whoever she is, we'd best find her soon. The weather is turning and if she is out in it..."

Good God, to think of her wandering senseless in the cold and the dark... it was too horrible. He wouldn't let himself think it.

"Come!"

He and the physician left the ice house, slamming the door shut. Where to start on their search for her? Their position was remote, his estate lands vast. She could be anywhere. He'd need a small army to search everywhere.

Fortunately, he had an idea just where to go find one. He could see their lights now, the wagon at the rear of his castle, dark outlines of men milling about. Drake had returned from his venture. They were successful, it seemed.

Pray God they'd be equally so in their search for Miss Horne. Or whoever she was.

Chapter 14

Cassandra was dizzy from not breathing. Mr. Rovish had her pressed into the corner, pinning her and clamping one hand over her mouth. She had lost one of the shawls, but huddled with the remaining one. The kitten still mewed and squirmed in Rovish's free hand. Every now and then in his struggles she could feel a tiny claw snag on her shawl, but she was helpless to give aid.

"Stow them in here, lads," a voice called as the looming, dark shadow of a man filled the cell doorway.

"Gentle, now," someone else called.

Then another form was in the doorway, then another. It seemed a whole trail of men were coming into the cell with them. Apparently it was dark enough to keep Cassandra and her captor hidden, and the incoming men were clearly preoccupied. She could not see well enough to make out details, but it seemed each man carried a bag. Not a huge bag, but a bag that appeared to wriggle on its own when it was placed carefully on the floor over on the far side of the cell.

She recoiled. Good heavens, what were these men doing? What could possibly be in those bags? And what would they do when they found her and Mr. Rovish hiding here, privy to their odd dealings?

She held her breath and waited.

"His lordship's going to think us all the go, the way we've carried this off without any hubble-bubble," one of the men said as he deposited his writhing, yelping bag.

"Don't go singing yer praises yet," another spoke up. "There's still time for this to go plenty to pieces."

A third lowered his bag and added, "Old Rovish is going to find out what we've done and we'll be laid by our heels."

She felt the younger Mr. Rovish stiffen at the sound of the name.

"Shut it," one of the men barked, silencing even the yelping for a moment. "Rovish ain't going to do nothing. 'Is lordship'll see we come out of this. He'll marry that wench then be all in high water. Things gets better when the purse gets fed, as they say."

"I hope so," the others muttered, expressing concern but at the same time clearly not eager to criticize their master.

So whatever illicit thing they were up to, Lord Braden was in on it. She could not be surprised, yet she could make little sense of it. If the earl hadn't been planning to kidnap her, if he wasn't on friendly terms or working in league with Mr. Rovish, what on earth was he doing?

"Have we got them all in here?" the man who seemed to be in charge called from the doorway.

"We do, sir," came the reply. "Now what?"

"Now we let them out of the bags."

No one spoke. Cassandra decided that was not a good sign.

"Er, how we going to keep 'em in here?"

"Everyone out, all but two of you," the leader said. "We'll keep the door shut and you let them all out. They'll likely go hide in a corner. Fearful little things, they are."

She began to think she recognized this as the voice of Braden's man, the one he'd been plotting with during the night. Indeed, it would make sense he should be heading this enterprise, whatever it was. But where was Lord Braden?

The men muttered and grumbled and eventually selected two to stay behind while the rest of them filed out of the cell. So far none of them had shone light in this particular corner and Cassandra began to worry they might not discover them at all. And just what fearful creatures were these that would soon be released from those bags? Heavens, but she and Mr. Rovish would be trapped in here with them if she didn't make her presence known quickly.

Yet Mr. Rovish seemed rather inclined to take his chances with the animals. He pinched her as a reminder of his threat. The kitten wheezed.

One of the men heard the sound and swung his half-shuttered lantern their direction. His partner, unfortunately, had not noticed and had gone ahead and opened the first bag. Everything became sudden chaos.

The man with the lantern noticed them and called out, which startled his companion and apparently caused him to jump, which frightened whatever it was that had been still in the bag. The creature came flying out, a yelping mass of reddish fur and sharp, nipping teeth. It snapped at the men—who responded with some yelping of their own—and dashed across the cell toward the corner where Cassandra was hidden.

Mr. Rovish yelped, as well, and threw the kitten at the advancing creature. Cassandra cried out, but the kitten was fast. He bounced off the snarling reddish form and came sailing back her way, latching onto her gown and climbing her like a tree. She pried his nails out of her skin and held him tightly, both for his own safety and hers. The other animal was too terrified to give chase, but lunged instead at Mr. Rovish with his teeth snapping and feet flailing across the cold, damp floor. Mr. Rovish shoved away from Cassandra and made for the doorway.

Lord Braden's men caught him there.

"What the hell is this?" the leader called.

"Get it away from me!" Mr. Rovish screeched, kicking out as if to defend himself from the animal.

But the animal, which turned out to be a small and very underfed fox, was not in the least bit interested in giving further attack. He had found the end of Cassandra's shawl drooping down onto the ground and had already burrowed himself under it, trying desperately to escape the madness around him. She could feel his slight form shaking and didn't dare move, lest he might be uncovered and feel threatened again.

"By the devil, it's young Rovish," the man with the lantern said, holding it up then turning to shine it on Cassandra. "And he's been wenching in our holding pen."

How revolting! She was quick to correct them.

"Not with me, he has not. I did not end up here of my own free will, I assure you."

Braden's man peered at her. "Miss Horne? What are you—"

He was interrupted by more shouting from the

corridor. She could hear footsteps racing, coming closer. The man holding the lantern swore, but then she recognized one of the approaching voices. Lord Braden!

"Drake!" he called, not yet into view and clearly not aware all that was happening here. "I need you to gather your men and come quickly. Miss Horne has gone missing!"

She rather liked the desperate tone in his voice, but of course that would be gone soon. He'd find her here and demand explanation. There'd be no way to deny things now, even if she wanted to. And indeed, a big part of her wanted to. But he deserved better. She'd confess to the truth and just pray he didn't turn her out with Mr. Rovish.

"I believe we have found her, sir," the man called Drake replied.

Instantly Lord Braden appeared in the doorway. At first his eyes caught on the man being held captive there.

"Rovish? What are you doing in my dungeon?"

But Mr. Rovish simply sneered at him then slid an accusing glance over at Cassandra. "Perhaps you should ask her."

Lord Braden looked at her. His eyes went huge and she was afraid what emotions she would see in them. But a smile quickly tugged at his lips and pushed past his man into the cell. She could almost feel his embrace, sense that he meant to swoop her up into his arms. Oh, how she wanted him to! Instead, though, she stopped him.

"Wait, my lord! I... er, I have a fox under my gown."

The terrified thing had crawled under her shawl, then under her gown, then wrapped itself snuggly around her ankles. She couldn't move if she'd wanted to, not without sending it into another panic. And this way perhaps she could have a moment to overcome her own sense of panic. How on earth was she going to look him in the eye and admit how she'd lied?

He seemed perplexed only for a moment, then glanced around the cell, taking in the situation.

"Sorry, my lord," one of his men said. "We didn't know they was in here and we let a fox out of its bag. Scared little thing, it is."

"I see," he replied, then smiled when he noticed the kitten in her arms. "Good thing it didn't notice that tasty treat you're holding. Very well, I'll retrieve the fox. If you'd be so kind, just stay still, Miss Horne."

Mr. Rovish laughed. "Miss Horne? Who the hell is Miss Horne?"

Drake tweaked his ear. "She's the young lady you were treating poorly, you cur. The one that his lordship is planning to marry."

Mr. Rovish snorted, so Drake pulled his stick away from him and whacked him on the back of the legs. Cassandra cringed as Mr. Rovish howled and hit the ground on his knees.

"We don't appreciate disrespect," Drake growled.

Lord Braden ignored it all and moved slowly toward Cassandra, tugging up her gown just enough to see the fox. It made a whining, whimpering sound, but did not bolt and send everyone into alarm as she feared. It simply huddled closer to her leg and then passively let Lord Braden wrap it into his cloak.

"The poor thing is in shock," he said softly. "Too

much for one day. We'll have to watch and make sure all of them are allowed quiet and calm after this. The sooner we can provide that, the better."

Mr. Rovish snorted as if such concern for mere foxes was a disgusting thing, but he held his peace quickly when Drake brandished that stick again. Lord Braden rose to his feet and handed the fox bundle to one of his men. And older gentleman Cassandra did not recognize moved into view in the doorway, but Lord Braden paid him no mind. He smiled at Cassandra and came back to her.

"You are free now?"

"Yes, my lord."

"Good."

He didn't hesitate to take her in his arms. She would have melted happily into him if she could have.

"Er, kitten, my lord," she muttered, shifting in his embrace.

He glanced down and smiled, still keeping his arms around her but careful not to crush the little thing. She wished with every part of her that she could stay this way, safe and warm in his arms, forever. Mr. Rovish, of course, was eager to ruin it all.

"I don't know who Miss Horne is, but you ought to know this little hussy ain't her."

Drake jabbed him with the stick, but the foul man merely chuckled through his pain. The damage was done. The words had been said and Lord Braden would expect explanation. She steeled herself to look up into his eyes.

"Is this true?" he asked gently.

"I'm sorry. I should never have lied to you, my lord. I was confused and afraid and... yes, it's true. I'm not really Miss Horne."

"I know."

"You know?"

"The good doctor informed me."

"Doctor?"

He released her slightly to turn and indicate the man in the doorway. She studied him, wondering if perhaps he did seem just a bit familiar. Did she know the man? He was studying her intently, and did not seem to be pleased with what he was seeing.

"She is not Miss Horne," the man announced.

"No, I am not," she acknowledged, though it was impossible to look Lord Braden in the eye again. "You've been so kind to me and I took advantage. I hope the real Miss Horne will arrive soon and you can be together."

"Good lord, I hope not," Lord Braden said. "Miss Horne is not at all the sort of person I want to spend the rest of my life with."

"But you asked her to marry you!"

He shook his head. "No, I asked *you* to marry me, as I recall. And you agreed."

"Well, yes, but... I was never actually going to go through with it! You wanted Miss Horne, not me. You told me yourself how well you were suited, how you had business with her father. He is wealthy, I presume, and must be a fine man. My father is... well..."

Mr. Rovish snorted again, and ducked before Drake's stick could make contact. "Yes, do tell him about your dear father!" he taunted.

She snapped at him. "My father is dead because of you! He might have been a base-born scoundrel, but he never deserved being murdered."

"Is this true?" Lord Braden asked.

She sighed. "Yes, it is. My father was not the most honorable man. He and Mr. Rovish were involved in a terrible scheme and I'm ashamed to admit they duped me into joining them."

"Yes, but your father was murdered? It was no accident that befell your carriage?"

"Oh, indeed that was an accident," she said, and hesitated to tell the full of it. It was her struggle with Rovish that caused the coachman to be shot, after all. Still, it was an accident. What Mr. Rovish did to Papa, though, was not. "But my father was dead long before our carriage careened off that hillside. He was poisoned. By Mr. Rovish."

Everyone glared at Mr. Rovish. She thought it quite telling that no one at all seemed to question her story. Each one of them appeared quite convinced the man was fully capable of what she accused.

"Don't cry like he's some sort of loss," Mr. Rovish snarled at her. "The man was willing to throw his own chit to the wolves for a bit of blow."

"He trusted you," she said. "He thought you would keep your end of the bargain, that no one would get hurt."

"Then he was a fool. What did he think I'd do with a tempting morsel like you? Give you back and just walk away? Even Braden's not fool enough to do that, it appears. Pity he wasn't enough for you and you had to come down here looking for me."

"I did not come looking for you!"

"Then why were you down here?"

Now she could feel everyone's glare upon her. Indeed, Mr. Rovish raised a good question. Lord

Braden would want to know why she'd come down here.

"I came down here to leave. I thought if I went away and no one knew how to find me, then none of my father's associates could, either. The real Miss Horne would arrive and Lord Braden could marry as he had planned."

"Well, fortunately that won't be happening," Lord Braden said. "You won't need to run from Mr. Rovish and Miss Horne won't be arriving."

"She won't? But... she plans to be married to you!"

"No, she plans to be married to her coachman, apparently. But come, let us get out of this damp. Drake, you can see to the rest of the foxes. Food and water for them right away."

"Indeed, sir. What of this baggage?" Drake poked Mr. Rovish with the stick.

"I suppose it won't do to leave it here," Lord Braden said, cocking his head. "Not good for the foxes. Give me two of your men and we'll find someplace to hold him. The magistrate will be very interested in speaking with him."

Lord Braden orchestrated the arrangements but kept her close to his side. She was happy enough to comply. There had been too many things to go wrong lately. She knew better than to try any further silly escape plans. Besides, the earl was a decent man. It seemed he would not toss her out into the cold even now that he knew the truth. With Mr. Rovish in custody and her conscience clear at last, she had nothing more to escape from.

In fact, leaving MacMorton Castle would feel nothing like escape. That would imply that she wanted to leave.

Chapter 15

She held onto the kitten as if it might save her.
Braden's heart ached for her. What must she have been
through, first to see her own father murdered, then to
have survived that horrific accident, and now to have
barely escaped Rovish in a dungeon? A lesser woman
would have swooned in a fit of vapors, or been beyond
comfort and wailing aloud.

This woman, however, was quietly sitting in his
office, huddled in the chair he'd placed near the fire and
cooing to an unnamed whelp of a cat. From what he
could gather, she handled herself remarkably well in the
dungeon. He'd never known Gilford Rovish to be a
rational man, yet she'd managed to escape him twice,
and this time saving a kitten along with her. And one
terrified fox kit, as well.

Remarkable woman, indeed.

"When will the magistrate be here?" the doctor
asked Braden, settling himself into a chair across from
his newest patient.

"I've decided to wait until morning to send for him,"
Braden replied, hoping it hadn't been too obvious that
he was staring with puppy-like longing at Miss Horne.
Or whatever her name was.

"Will you be able to keep that man contained?"

"Mr. Rovish seems to have been through quite a lot. I doubt he'll be running off on us," Braden replied. "However, I've instructed my servants to keep him locked in his room and I've placed footmen outside his door."

"He was injured in the accident," the young lady said quietly. "I thought he'd been killed. I was surprised when Lord Braden made no mention of him."

"It seems he made his way out to the hunting box, licking his wounds and waiting to learn if anyone was out searching for him. He saw my men spying on the place earlier today, and that is why he followed them back here and hid in my dungeon."

"I should never have suspected you to be in league with him. I mistook what I heard that night in the corridor and assumed the worst of you."

"A mistake anyone might have made," he assured her. "How could you have guessed what Drake and I were really planning? It was natural for you to be concerned."

"If I had not suspected you, though, I could have told the truth. You could have been on the alert for Mr. Rovish. There is no telling what he might have done, prowling about your home unnoticed," she said.

"You have offered more than enough apology, my dear. You had no way of knowing who you could or could not trust. As it is, you saved us quite a bit of trouble, actually."

"I did? How on earth do you figure that?"

"With young Rovish in my custody accused of murder and abduction, his father will not be so hasty to go to war with me now. Without your testimony, we would never have known what he did."

"But how does that make his father less likely to feud?"

"You've given me leverage, my dear. Old Mr. Rovish is the one I stole those poor foxes from. He caught them on my lands and had planned to turn them loose for a hunt."

"Turn them loose? But the poor thing that I saw was so small and so frail. Has the man not fed them? How could they possibly be any sport?"

"Exactly my feeling on the matter, my dear. I tried to convince him to sell them to me, but the man would not go for my price. The hunt is scheduled for tomorrow, which is why Drake and I had to act now. I had men traveling to and from the hunting box daily to make certain the foxes were well and to set plans for our, er, rescue. We had no idea young Rovish was there. It seems he followed the scout party back, looking to report to his father whatever dastardly deed I was about. When you found him and distracted him, actually, you saved me from that. Now when old Rovish gets word of the foxes, he will hardly be able to balk, seeing as his son is a suspect of murder and was found in my home abducting a lady."

"You are trying to make me feel better, I think," she said, but tipped her face up just enough to give him a smile.

"I am making myself feel better, actually. I was not looking forward to ending up in court over a pack of half-starved foxes. But, if you are feeling better after your ordeal, then I am quite happy."

"You did a noble thing, sir. I am glad you won't end up in jail."

"It would be highly unlikely for an earl to be jailed

over something like this," the doctor said in all seriousness. "They were your own foxes, after all. It's more likely the old Rovish fellow could be held up on charges for stealing them from you in the first place."

"Well, it seems the only one facing charges now is the one who really deserves it," Braden said. "And the foxes are saved."

"What will you do with them?" she asked.

"Fatten them, teach them to fend for themselves, then put them back in the wild where they belong."

"That is a good thing, my lord," she said, but he detected a yawn.

"You are exhausted," he said. "I'll call Mrs. Garver to take you up to your bed."

"But... surely you have more questions for me, after all that has happened?"

"I think questions can wait until morning, don't you?"

He could see that she fought back another yawn. "I suppose, sir."

"Would you like me to make up something to help you to sleep?" the physician offered.

She wrinkled her nose at that thought. "No, thank you, sir. I believe after my day I'll fall asleep without effort."

"Very well, but do call for me if you need anything," the man said. "I've come a long way, so I might as well make myself useful."

She thanked him very nicely then rose when the housekeeper appeared at the door.

"I think our day has been long enough," Braden announced. "Mrs. Garver, would you see that the young lady is made comfortable? And we'll need a room prepared for Dr. Morrow, as well."

"Of course, sir. Come, my dear," she said, taking the young lady's arm. "Do you suppose we could send the kitten back to its mother?"

"Oh, let her keep it with her tonight, Mrs. Garver," Lord Braden said. "Send up the mother and the rest of the litter, too. I think they could all use each other's company tonight."

His beautiful guest gave him another smile, this one more brilliant than that last.

"Thank you, sir," she said. "I would like that."

Mrs. Garver clucked her tongue and shook her head, but Braden knew her enough to recognize a smile hidden beneath that stern, motherly expression. She would take good care of his mystery lady. They would become good friends.

At least, he sincerely hoped the young miss was here long enough for that. He supposed he ought to find out if he had any reason to hope. For all he knew, she could have a family of her own off somewhere.

Now that she was safe from any outside threat, she might truly be ready to leave. He would have to ask her about this. But not now. Tonight she needed some rest. There would be time for his many questions in the morning.

Yes, he could wait until morning. Perhaps he should savor this last night of ignorance. There was no telling what he might learn of his lady. She might, in fact, belong to someone else. Indeed, he could wait his whole lifetime before learning that. One answer, though, could simply not wait.

"One question first, Miss," he called just before Mrs. Garver led her from the room.

She turned with a puzzled look. "Yes, my lord?"

"Your name."

She smiled. Apparently this was a question she could answer with ease.

"Cassandra Loring, sir."

By God, what a beautiful name.

"Good night, then, Miss Loring."

"Thank you, sir. To you, too."

He tried not to grin like an idiot but was fairly certain he failed. She turned back to him and made his stomach turn flips.

"And thank you. For everything."

"You are quite welcome, my dear."

And then she left with Mrs. Garver. He stared after them, almost not hearing the doctor.

"Hmm. Loring. Why does that sound familiar?"

"Er, do you know her?"

The older man shrugged. "Most likely not. Pretty girl like that, I'm sure I would recall her."

Indeed, Braden knew it was unlikely he'd ever forget her. He had her name now, too. One other important thing, as well. She'd not corrected him when he said "Miss". That, more than everything, was the best news of the day.

Morning dawned bright and clear. Cassandra woke early feeling restless and anxious. What would Lord Braden do with her today? She didn't know quite what she hoped for. She had no right to hope for anything, of course.

He was a good man, a kind man. He would probably not order her to leave. She would have to be the one to suggest it. With luck he would give her transport, and help her arrange to have father carried home, as well. Grandmother would resent it, to have him in the family plot, but for Cassandra she'd allow it. After all, Mr. Rovish was the real villain. Papa was just a sad little man who'd never gotten over his wife's death. Surely Grandmother could have pity on that.

She paced about her room, playing with the kittens as they scampered about, but she could not be content. It was early, but perhaps Braden was downstairs already. She called for a servant to come help her dress, made sure the cat family got removed to the pantry to be given some breakfast, and hurried to the morning room.

It must have been later than she thought. Breakfast was laid out on the sideboard and Braden was at table with Dr. Morrow. She paused in the doorway. The man's brute of a dog lay contentedly at his feet, but raised his big head and thumped his tail on the floor when he spotted Cassandra.

Oh, but this sight would be too easy to get used to. The sunlight streamed in from the east, lighting the room and settling on his lordship in a warm hazy glow. Unearthly voices sang songs of rejoicing somewhere in the distance. Or perhaps she was imagining that bit. Still, there was no denying the man made a fine figure.

"Miss Loring!" he called when he saw her. "Good morning. Do join us."

The doctor added his greetings as well. "We were just saying how we hoped you passed a good night."

"Yes, I did. Thank you."

"Come, sit," Lord Braden said, leaving his chair to present her with one nearest to him.

He signaled to a servant who made quick work of putting together a plate for Cassandra. It was a good deal more than she would have selected on her own, but perhaps she ought to force herself to eat a bit more than usual. The last few days her nerves had been on edge and her appetite had been nearly nonexistent.

Then again, her nerves were not exactly calm and serene today. How on earth was she going to eat, feeling as if a flock of pigeons fluttered here and there through her insides? And with Lord Braden watching her, smiling at her... indeed, that did nothing to calm her and did everything to set the pigeons soaring.

"I had cook send up some chocolate. Will you take some, Miss Loring?" he asked, offering a cup.

"Yes, thank you."

"And you will note I remembered your name."

Her face went hot. Indeed, it must be confusing for him to have to relearn her name. He likely felt as if he did not know her at all. She truly did not deserve such kindness from him today, yet the dear man had given her chocolate. The best she could do for him was to leave here as quickly as possible.

"I hope you will not be forced to remember it long, sir."

She stared at the food on her plate rather than glance over to see how he might take that. With relief, most likely, and that would be hard for her to see. That he might wish her to leave pained her, yet of course she knew she could never blame him. The sooner she got this over with, the better.

She struggled to hide the churning anguish inside when he replied.

"Yes, I hope for that, too."

"I... I should send word of what's happened back to my grandmother," she sipped the chocolate for what comfort it could give her. "She must be quite worried, of course."

"Of course. The weather is clearing today so my servants should have no difficulty at all posting a letter."

"And perhaps you might suggest how I can arrange to have Papa's body removed for home?"

"Is that what you wish? He should be buried in London?"

"No sir. London is not my home."

"Of course. I forget that everything I know about you is now false."

Oh, but did he have to remind her so constantly of her deception? She tried not to show her discomfort. He need never know how much she cared for him or for his estimation.

"I am from Lincolnshire, sir," she said, choosing to seem unaffected.

"Lovely area," the doctor commented, helping himself to the jam. "I have visited there upon occasion."

"Lincolnshire? But that's merely a day's journey from here," Lord Braden commented.

"A difficult day's journey, yes."

"Not so difficult in good weather, and with the right company, Miss Loring."

She had to agree with that. Indeed, traveling here in bad weather with the likes of Mr. Rovish most assuredly made the day far more difficult that it should have been. She was not looking forward to her return trip, however. How lonely it would be, with Papa in a box and she on her own.

"It will be good to return to familiar surroundings," she said, hoping it sounded cheerful.

"I'm sure that it will. But... I hope you will allow me to accompany you."

"What? Oh, there is no need for that, sir. I'm sure I'll be fine on the mail coach."

"Mail coach? Is that how you wish to travel?"

"Surely there is a village somewhere near here where I can get passage?"

"Yes, of course but... Miss Loring, I would much rather you use my carriage. It's not the finest available, but I assure you it's serviceable. You'd be far safer that way."

"I couldn't let you put yourself out! Truly, the mail coach is fine."

"If that's what you wish, but you should not go alone. I'm sure Mrs. Garver would—"

"No! Oh heavens, I couldn't possibly force her to travel halfway across the country like that."

"Then me. Please allow me—"

"You cannot, my lord. Really, you've been more than kind, but..."

"But what? You are so eager to be rid of me that you'd rather endanger yourself?"

"I doubt there's much danger in traveling via mail coach."

"It's just that... you've been through so much already. I can't imagine you'd wish to put yourself through more."

As if traveling with him would not be putting herself through more anguish! Or perhaps he doubted that she'd truly head home. Perhaps he half expected her to stop off along the way and insinuate herself into some other man's home, to lie her way into further kind treatment or hot chocolate.

"I will be fine on my own," she insisted, the decided she couldn't stomach more breakfast. "If you please, I'm not hungry, my lord. I think I should go write that letter for my grandmother."

She got up from the table, the men quickly matching her movement to rise in respect. They needn't have bothered. She planned to be out of this room and away from their presence in less than a moment. She had to. She would not be able to hold back the tears for any longer than that.

The dog's tail thumped the floor again as she left. Fitting, she thought. Even the hound was glad to see the last of her. No doubt it would be good for things here to get back to normal. She made it out to the corridor and found a quiet niche in a window overlooking the stream that acted as moat and the mist-covered hillsides that rolled out beyond. Tears half blinded her to the beauty of it all, though, and it was a shame. She wanted to etch every inch of MacMorton into her memory for the lonely days no doubt to come.

But she would not let herself be overcome here. It was time to do what was needed and to hold on to some bit of her dignity. She wiped back the tears with one hand, and clutched a fist at her side with the other. The cold, wet dog nose that suddenly pressed into it was quite startling, to say the least.

"Brutus thought you might need this," Lord Braden's voice said behind her.

Drat. He'd followed her and now he'd found her here, crying. What an utter ninny he must think her by now. Yet when she turned to face him, his expression was still kind, still so caring.

He offered her a handkerchief, so she took it.

"Brutus also thinks I'm a beast for upsetting you," he added.

"No, you're not a beast," she assured him. "You've been nothing but kind and I've lied and deceived you. And Brutus."

"Have you?" he asked. "When have you lied?"

"I told you that I was Miss Horne."

"No, we just assumed that was your name because *you* turned up when we expected *her*."

"I could have corrected you."

"You feared for your life."

"I should have admitted the truth."

"And now you have, unless... are there other lies you should confess to me?"

"Er, no."

"Good. Because today is Christmas and I think even your father—rest his soul—would want you to be jolly."

"I'm sorry, but I don't feel very jolly."

"Yes, I can see that. Come, there's something I want to show you."

He took her by the hand and didn't give her time to refuse. Brutus followed as they went to end of the corridor and rounded the corner into the grand ballroom. There he stopped, allowing her to gape at the scene set before her.

The decorating was complete. Lively greens hung at every window and candles were lit, even in the bright light of day. When he pointed her toward the corner, she was quite surprised. A yew tree had been brought in, covered with bright parcels in colored paper, and morsels of fruit and some sweets. She'd seen engravings of the like, but never seen it herself.

"You have a Christmas tree!"

"My mother was German," he said. "While she lived, this was our tradition. The castle would be full of festivities, with friends and with dancing. I believe Christmas was her favorite of times."

"And you've not celebrated since she's been gone?"

"Well... not in a grand way. My father was not a good man, I'm sorry to say. He cared little for home or for family. Once my mother was gone, he banned all festive behaviors. No greenery, no gifting, and certainly no Christmas tree."

"That's so sad for you. You were just a child, weren't you?"

"I was. But I wasn't unloved. Mrs. Garver took me on as her own. With my father gone most of the time, I was allowed to exist quite serenely, as a matter of fact. The servants, the tenants... they were my family. When I left here for school, they were the people I longed for, not my father. Then, unexpectedly, I inherited the title and came home. To stay, I had hoped."

"MacMorton is beautiful. I can see why you love it."

"I do. But there are times when... Well, as you are aware, it is rather remote."

"But if you are happy here, that should make little difference."

"I agree. It makes no difference at all to me, but to others, well... Miss Loring, when you told me you were pleased with MacMorton, that you wished to know it as your own, were you lying to me then?"

She tried to turn away from him, but he wouldn't let

her. Apparently the man truly did insist on full honesty now. Well then, that's what he would have, no matter how foolish it would make her look. She met his eyes and took a deep breath.

"No, my lord. I was not lying."

"Even though it is crumbling and filled up with badgers and foxes and servants who sometimes forget I'm an earl?"

"I think especially because of all that, my lord. It feels like... a home."

"It is, Miss Loring. I'd like it to be *your* home."

She refused to let herself comprehend. She must have heard wrong.

"You're not saying anything," he noted.

"I don't know what to say."

"Then perhaps I should rephrase my question."

She blinked in astonishment as he led her into the center of the room, under a gaily decorated bough his servants had done up with greens and with holly, and then dropped to one knee before her. The huge room suddenly became quite stuffy, the air mysteriously gone as she struggled to catch her breath. He took her hands in his and gazed up at her.

"Miss Cassandra Loring, I'm not a wealthy man. I've got very little to offer but a tumble-down castle and a 200 year old title, but I can give you my heart. Will you please do me the great honor of at least considering making MacMorton your home... and me your husband?"

She couldn't speak. She could barely stand. He was asking for her, in earnest! He did not even know who she was, not really, yet he was asking to marry her. It was all she could do not to accept him right there and then hold him to it later when he came to his senses.

She was trying quite desperately to think of any good reason to refuse him. It seemed the right thing to do, considering how little he knew her, of course. He was an earl, after all, and deserved someone whose father had not been a petty criminal, murdered on the road. He was likely only asking her out of a sense of duty, or for pity. She could never let him marry for pity.

Then again, he had offered more than just his hand. He'd offered his heart. Had he meant it? That was a gift she could never turn down. After all, she'd already given him hers.

"Are you very certain you want me?" she asked.

"I am."

"Completely certain?"

"Enormously certain."

Oh, but she did like the sound of that.

"In that case, sir—"

But she was cut off by a scream. Then a string of words such as she'd once heard her father use when he'd been stepped on by a horse. They came from the corridor, or perhaps even another room.

"The breakfast room," Lord Braden said.

"Good heavens!"

Whatever happened, it must have been quite dreadful to cause someone to shout out in that manner. Lord Braden leapt to his feet.

"I'm sorry. I should see to this."

"Yes... of course," she replied.

He dropped her hands and rushed away. She could have cried from disappointment. What if he did come to his senses? He might never allow her the chance to give her reply! He might not wish for her answer.

But he turned back to her. The anguished swearing had subsided, though deep muttering still echoed throughout. He would have to attend it, there was no doubt. But at least he took one single moment to spare her some parting words.

"We *will* resume this discussion, Miss Loring."

"I... er, yes."

But he stalked from the room without realizing she'd not been simply agreeing. She had given her answer. Heaven help her if something awful occurred and ruined the moment. As Papa's sudden demise had taught her, sometimes moments are never to be recaptured.

Chapter 16

What the devil were all these interruptions? Would he never get the opportunity to properly court the woman he intended to marry? How on earth did every other man in England manage to find a way when he'd met nothing but obstacle after obstacle?

However, if someone was screeching in agony somewhere in his castle, it was his responsibility to see to it and rectify the problem. Then perhaps he could get back to properly proposing to Miss Loring. *Cassandra.* Lord, but he certainly preferred this name to Philberta. Actually, he preferred everything about Miss Loring to what he knew of the other young lady.

Perhaps someday he'd finally get the chance to tell her about it without constant distraction.

"What is it?" he called, rushing into the morning room, which turned out indeed to be the source of the shouting.

"Bloody thing sticks like a pincushion!"

Dr. Morrow stood at the sideboard, his plate of food forgotten as he dabbed at a trickle of blood on his fingers. He grumbled some unpleasant words while from under the cabinet a loud and very ill-tempered chuffing could be heard. Braden recognized it immediately.

"Ah, you found Mr. Prickles. I wondered where he'd gone off to."

The doctor looked at him as if he were loony, but Miss Loring came rushing into the room just then and drew his attention.

"What happened?" she called breathlessly.

"I dropped my spoon," Dr. Morrow said, nearly as ill-tempered as the chuffing. "It went under the sideboard. When I reached down to get it, I got viciously stabbed."

"You were stabbed?" She looked horrified.

"Not stabbed," Braden was quick to clarify. "Pricked is all."

"Pricked by a hundred of the ruddy sharpest needles ever. What the devil have you under there, Braden?"

The earl could not condone the use of such language around a young lady, but he'd run afoul of Mr. Prickles before. He allowed the good doctor a moment of lapsed civility.

"It's a hedgehog, sir."

He took up a towel and stooped to peer under the sideboard. Indeed, there was Mr. Pickles, a spiky, brown ball of disgruntled insectivore. Careful to avoid the good doctor's fate, Braden rolled the small creature into the towel and drew him out from his hiding spot. He held the animal in a soft, secure bundle and returned to his feet. The chuffing faded to an occasional huff.

"You've got a hedgehog in there?" Miss Loring asked.

"He generally prefers the garden, but an unfortunate accident left him in need of attention, so I've kept him indoors 'til he's well. By the sounds of it, he seems well enough now."

"I say, Braden, how unconventional! A hedgehog roaming free in your breakfast room?" the doctor said.

"He ordinarily thinks the breakfast room too bright," Braden said. "His usual haunt has been the blue drawing room in the rear of the living areas. It gets less sun."

He realized how foolish he must sound, presupposing to comprehend the ambient light preferences of a mere hedgehog, and a quite grumpy one, at that. But one glance at Miss Loring convinced him she did not think so. She seemed completely at ease with all of this. Of course he *should* have a hedgehog in his breakfast room. Just as he *should* have Miss Loring for bride.

"He must have been sleeping, and was startled when you reached for the spoon," she said, as she turned to the doctor. "Have you been wounded very badly?"

In the face of the young lady's concern, the physician seemed to feel foolish for his outburst. "I was not wounded by a... a hedgehog. He pricked me, is all. I daresay I will recover."

"Would you like me to look at it?" she asked. "Perhaps Lord Braden has some salve or a dressing on hand."

"I am a physician, miss, I do not need..." but his indignant words tapered away and he was now looking at Miss Loring with a curious expression. "I say, you are Cassandra Loring?"

"I am sir," she said, then glanced at Braden with her own curious expression.

Now the doctor broke into a smile. "Good heavens, I recall you now! My, but it's been ages; you were just a slip of a thing."

"You know me, sir?"

"Indeed, I know your grandmother. I treated her for a year when she was in Bath."

"Oh, heavens, yes! I remember you now! I thought I had seen you before. Indeed, that was nearly five years ago when we were staying in Bath, sir."

"Has it been so long? Tell me, how is your dear grandmother?"

"Quite well, sir, thank you. She still battles the gout, but to be honest, it only seems to plague her when my uncle insists she visit him and my cousins at their home in London."

The doctor laughed, and shared a remembrance of his experience with Miss Loring's grandmother. Miss Loring laughed and mentioned something she recalled from their Bath days. Braden felt very much left out. Just who was this Miss Loring that Dr. Morrow should have treated her grandmother and cavorted with many of the high nobilities whose names he so casually mentioned as associates? Miss Loring seemed to know every one of them.

"You are acquainted with Lord Colsworth?" Braden said, inserting himself into the conversation when it touched on someone familiar.

"Indeed," Miss Loring replied. "His mother is some sort of cousin to my Grandmother. Do you know him?"

"I was at school with him. A cousin, you say?"

She wrinkled her nose, deep in thought. "Somewhere along the line. I've not been in company with him much, but when we are in London my Grandmother usually receives him."

"And are you often in London?" He almost dreaded the answer.

"As infrequently as possible," she replied, seemingly unaware how she had just brightened his day. "Neither my Grandmother nor I are much enamored by city life, I'm afraid. I'm sure it sounds silly, but I very much prefer the country."

"I don't think it sounds silly at all, Miss Loring. I quite comprehend."

"I thought that you might," she said, gracing him with one of her enchanting smiles.

Their eyes caught for a moment and he was only too happy to let everything else fade around them. The moment was interrupted, of course. By the doctor again.

"Perhaps you are unaware of Miss Loring's identity, my lord?"

Perhaps he was. True, he knew she was the only women who could ever bring him true happiness, but obviously there was much more to her. He ought to at least find out the name of her grandmother.

"I'm afraid I am a bit in the dark," he admitted.

"Her grandmother is Lady Wythelea, daughter of the Duke of Merle."

What was this? Miss Loring was not only gently bred, but great-granddaughter of a duke? Even Braden had to go a few generations back to find such an illustrious patent in his lineage. How on earth could he have not known this of her? He should have guessed merely by the way that she carried herself, the way that she spoke.

She could do far better than him. He should have known that.

"I'm sorry," he said. "If I went into society more often I'm sure I would have met your fine grandmother."

"And she would tell you all about her gout, I'm sure," Miss Loring replied. ""And if you are wise, you will pretend to listen intently, or else she's liable to tell you again."

"She is a fine woman and a pleasure to attend," the doctor said. "Lord Braden, you will like her immensely."

Braden could answer to that in full earnestness. "I hope I get opportunity."

"As do I, my lord," Miss Loring replied. "She would wish to keep you with her forever."

"I'd be happy to oblige her, as long as you were with her, as well."

"I would stay anywhere you were, my lord."

"Then my joy would be complete."

The conversation lagged, but he did not break off staring at her. She was still smiling and he was convinced the earth itself had ceased turning. Her eyes held all the emotion and hope that he felt in his own heart. He could almost believe nothing existed outside of them and this great, warm bond that had drawn them together.

He moved closer to her. She moved closer to him. The clock on the mantle ticked in time with his heartbeat. The physician cleared his throat.

"You'd best give me the hedgehog if you intend to kiss her now, lad."

Since he actually did intend to kiss her, he handed the bundle over. The chuffing started up again, but Braden barely heard it. He did notice the doctor's chuckles, though. And the quick, meaningful glance he made up toward the ceiling.

Braden shifted his eyes to see just what the good man had noticed. There, hanging on a bit of red ribbon all tied with a bow was a ball of fresh mistletoe his servants must have found and brought in. Indeed, this was perfect.

Miss Loring glanced up to notice it and her cheeks went all pink again.

"We can't argue with tradition, my dear," he said, reaching for her before something else interrupted.

Dr. Morrow had the good sense to leave.

He kissed her beneath the mistletoe! Somehow she was sure he'd not needed that bit of dangling shrubbery to encourage him, though. And she was glad of it. It saved her the trouble of having to kiss him herself.

"I'm not done asking you to marry me, you know," he said at last. "I'm going to simply keep asking until you say yes."

"If this is how you ask, sir, I may be tempted to never give answer."

"Perhaps we can bargain, then."

"You would bargain with kisses? I must say, I rather like the sound of that."

"Good, since unfortunately that is all I can bargain with. To be honest, my dear, you deserve far better than me. I'm not well connected, I lead a dull life in a remote part of the country, and I'm practically penniless. Would to God I had more to offer you."

"But you're kind and you're clever and you've made me completely fall in love with you! What more could I want?"

"Two shillings to rub together?"

She slid her arms more tightly around him. "Silly man. What fun is it to rub shillings?"

Indeed, she could think of far better things for that. By his grin it seemed he could, as well.

"Besides," she added. "Once you marry me, you'll be quite wealthy indeed. My mother may have wed far below her, but my grandparents always looked out for me. I come with quite a large fortune, you know. Would you like me to tell you about it?"

"Not in the least, my dear. Not in the least."

Which was exactly the answer she wanted. There'd be plenty of time to discuss her fortune and all the many things they might do with it. Right now, however, it was Christmas Day and there was mistletoe to be dutifully obeyed.

So they did. Repeatedly.

Note from Author:

I hope you enjoyed reading Yuletide Lies as much as I enjoyed the writing. It was fascinating to research some of the common Christmas traditions from that era. Often we hear that Christmas trees were introduced to England during the Victorian era, however there are plenty of contemporary references that assure us the Christmas Tree custom was alive and growing in England already in Regency times. In large part, this was due to the German heritage of Queen Charlotte who included Christmas Trees in royal celebrations as early as 1800. The English nobility were eager to emulate their monarch, and of course eventually the gentry and lower classes followed suit. And aren't we glad that they did?

Please visit my website at www.SusanGH.com to find out about my other Regency Historical Romance titles. Also, you can friend me on Facebook or other social media. I love to hear from readers!

*Keep reading for a preview of the next Regency
Romance coming soon from Susan Gee Heino...*

MISS FARROW'S FEATHERS
Susan Gee Heino

Meg Farrow choked on a feather. Handy, since she
needed one just now. She'd heard that passing a feather
through flame provided just the right odor to rouse an
insensible swooner. Poor insensible Mrs. Sedley-Stone
certainly did need rousing just now. She'd swooned—
but good—and the smelling salts hadn't worked.

It was just as well, though, considering that the very
uproar that had sent the woman into hysterics was still
roaring along. Or *soaring*, rather. Papa lunged about the
drawing room waving a net while the large, yellow-
headed parrot squawked loudly from atop the window
cornice where it had come to rest. Their usually
unflappable housekeeper screeched from the far corner,
flapping her arms twice as much as the bird.

Meg's head was beginning to throb. Two weeks of
this had been more than any of them could take.

"Bartholomew! Come down here right now," Papa
ordered, shaking his fist—his fist!—at the bright-eyed
parrot.

The bird cocked his head, ruffled his feathers, then
let Papa know exactly what he thought of that idea.
Heavens, but this creature knew words Meg had never
even heard before—and she spoke three languages. On

the settee, Mrs. Sedley-Stone had just begun to stir. Apparently she *did* know some of these words, because they made her swoon all over again.

"Watch your ruddy language, you bone-headed devil," Papa shouted at the bird.

"Papa, for heaven's sake," Meg chided.

Gracious, now even Papa had been corrupted by the parrot's influence. What were they to do? The whole village was talking about it. Innocent passers-by could not come within a hundred yards of their house but they were accosted by the most egregious verbiage, uttered loud and clear in a high-pitched raspy voice. It filtered through the doors, through the windows, out into the street. Anyone who didn't know better would think this was not the parsonage, but a common wharf-side alehouse.

Those who did know better would likely not have bothered coming so near to begin with. Sadly, Bartholomew's saucy tongue was well known in the community. Even sadder, it used to be contained to Glenwick Downs, a good two miles out of town. Now that their dear old friend, the Earl of Glenwick, had passed from this life and gone to his reward, Bartholomew had passed into the Farrow's possession and into the confines of the parsonage.

With him came the language. And the squawking. And the random feathers strewn all about the house. And other miscellaneous unfortunate things, the least of which was the swooning Mrs. Sedley-Stone. Meg was doing what she could to remedy all of these.

The insistent pounding at their front door did not help matters. When it was clear their housekeeper was far too preoccupied with being terrified of the parrot to tend to the arduous task of answering the door, Meg took a deep breath and abandoned Mrs. Sedley-Stone. It wasn't as if she would notice, after all, considering she was unconscious again.

Meg left the small drawing room and the chaos it contained. Of course the sound of Papa's bellowing and the bird's corresponding profanity were little diminished by the distance between her and the entry way. It would take far more than fifteen feet and one simple wall to stifle all that.

Most likely this was the very reason for all the pounding. She expected to find the local magistrate at their door, here to fine them for causing such a disturbance. Or perhaps word of their new house guest's unchristian-like behaviors had reached a higher authority and this pounding was to bring word from the Archbishop, threats against Papa if he didn't reform the dreadful bird right away. Most likely, though, it was one of their long-suffering neighbors with a hatchet and a sudden craving for exotic poultry. At this point, she would half welcome that.

In any case, it would be of little benefit to keep the insistent pounder waiting on the other side of that door. She patted her hair back into place, took a deep breath to calm her frayed nerves, then opened the door. Wisely, she took care to step back just in case there truly should be a hatched involved.

There was not.

Nor was there a magistrate, Archbishop, or any close neighbor. There was, in fact, no person she'd ever seen before. The gentleman she found at her door was quite clearly a stranger.

Not that he looked strange; quite the opposite, in

fact. This particular gentleman looked perfectly ordinary. He had all the requisite features, arranged in what most would consider a pleasing manner, and he wore very adequate clothing. They suited his elegant form quite well, as a matter of fact. His hat perched just right atop his head, which Meg couldn't help but notice was a good six feet off the ground, and his eyes were very much an agreeable shade of blue. Indeed, nothing at all strange about this man.

What was strange, however, was that he stood at her door appearing completely unruffled by all the ruckus in the background—as well as by her unseemly staring. In fact, while the housekeeper screeched and Papa sermonized behind her, this gentleman gave her a smile. Then he surprised her by speaking her name.

"Miss Farrow, I presume?"

Maxwell Shirley knew from the young lady's eyes—rather fetching brown eyes, as a matter of fact—that he'd guessed correctly. Miss Farrow, indeed. Then again, it was hardly a guess. He'd been told the Reverend Mr. Farrow lived at this home with a small staff and an adult daughter. And the parrot, of course.

Since the fresh-faced, demure young woman who answered the door could hardly be the staff—or the parrot—he felt it safe to presume she was Miss Farrow. She was just as he'd been told; well-dressed, lovely, and perfectly proper from top to bottom. Or so she would seem.

Max gave her a warm smile that had served him well with proper-seeming young ladies before. She responded by blinking those wide nut-brown eyes at him. Excellent. Perhaps this part of his journey would prove every bit as productive as he hoped. He was about to launch into the carefully benign greeting he had prepared.

His speech, however, was interrupted. A most distracting uproar came from the rooms behind her. Except for the slightest twitch in her left eye, she did a remarkable job of ignoring it, though.

"Er, yes. I am Miss Farrow," she answered him sweetly. "May I help you, sir?"

He cleared his throat, ready to get on with what might prove to be an uncomfortable interaction.

"Yes, I hope so, miss. I'm here to see..." he glanced at the paper in his hand and tried to appear charmingly awkward. "Mr. Farrow, I believe."

A crash sounded from somewhere inside. This time Miss Farrow appeared concerned and glanced over her shoulder. "I'm afraid he's—"

But a man's voice called from behind her. "I'm right here. Is there someone at the door?"

"Yes, Papa," she said, turning and pulling the door open wider as she did so.

Max could now see the parts of Miss Farrow's delightful form that had been hidden by the door. Delightful, indeed. He could also see the modest but carefully polished woodwork of an average-sized entrance way, along with a rather stiff, red-faced gentleman who, for some reason, was clutching a net. The unnatural shrieks and squawking from the interior of the house continued, though with slightly less fervor than at first.

"May I help you, sir?" Mr. Farrow said, puffing his way through the house to stand beside his daughter.

Max decided he'd do well to forget—at least for now, anyway—the young lady's delightfulness. It was time to be merely charming and eloquent. Perhaps he might find opportunity for delightfulness later on.

"I hope you may help me," he said to the man. "I am here to speak with you on a most important matter."

It was likely a waste of breath. Mr. Farrow wrinkled his brow in confusion. The man clearly had not heard a word Max had said, thanks to the uproarious squawking that echoed from another room in the house. A stream of impressive profanity accompanied the squawking. Max's ears perked to the chaotic din and it might just be about time to ask after it—as any normal person probably would—when a middle-aged woman in an apron came running out of a doorway and into the entrance hall, hands flailing over her head in a most Methodist manner. Quite unconventional, to say the least.

Indeed, though, it was quite welcome. All of this further convinced Max he'd come to the right place today. Miss Farrow clearly possessed the attributes to do what he suspected she'd done, while the good Reverend Farrow was obviously in possession of what Max had been seeking. Now Max was going to find out just what else these questionable clerics possessed... or how honestly they'd come by it.

"I have some questions for you," Max continued loudly, once the profanity had waned and the moaning Methodist had disappeared into the rear of the house.

"Questions about what?" the gentleman asked, leaning in toward Max in an effort to hear him clearly.

"I was told you were the person I needed to speak with about—" Max began to explain, but had to stop.

A large green and yellow bird suddenly sailed through the doorway that had just produced the flailing woman. It landed gracefully on the older man's shoulder and cocked his head, gazing with round, red eyes at Max. A parrot. By God, it was *the* parrot. Max smiled.

"Er, was that your parrot making all the fuss, sir?" Miss Farrow blushed. Mr. Farrow cleared his throat.

"What? Oh, er, well... yes, and I apologize if—"

The bird slapped him in the face with his wing as he leaped off the reverend's shoulder. It was too sudden for Max to do anything but stand stock still as the bird aimed straight for him and settled itself onto his shoulder, digging in his claws and brushing up against Max's hat. It slid downward over his eyes.

Max reached for the bird, pushing him aside just enough to right his hat, The bird uttered a moderately tame curse. Max tried to hide his pleasure. So the old bird remembered him, did he? Good for him. Now if Max could but trust that his only nice coat would not suffer some unlaunderable defacement.

As it turned out, however, his ear was the item in most immediate danger. The bird nibbled it and Max swore involuntarily. Damn. Not the best way to ingratiate himself into the good minister's favor. It did, however, seem to garner some sympathy from Miss Farrow. She waved her hand at the bird, trying to distract him from his very intent ear nibbling.

"I'm so sorry, sir," she said. "He has a preoccupation with ears, I'm afraid."

"I assure you," Max said, gently swiping at the bird. "I'm not opposed to a little ear nibble every now and again."

But he had little time to consider how Miss Farrow might take his admission. Instead of his swipes succeeding in removing the bird, they merely served to gain its attention. Max was rewarded by a two toed grip around his finger. The bird stepped up onto his hand and allowed Max to bring him round to eye level. Miss Farrow gasped. Mr. Farrow cleared his throat again. The bird cocked his head in the opposite direction and stared into Max's eyes.

Good old Bartholomew. How long had it been? A dozen years at least. And clearly the bird's vocabulary hadn't improved one bit.

"Good gracious," Mr. Farrow exclaimed. "You've tamed him!"

"Er, he's not actually a bad creature," Max said, then wondered if it was wise to give so much away already. "At least, so he would seem."

"You know parrots?" Mr. Farrow questioned.

In truth, Max knew nothing of parrots in general. He did, however know *this* one. Hell, he'd learned much from old Bartholomew in his younger days. After a bad night at the gaming table or a disappointing day at the races, he was rather thankful for the colorful descriptors he'd gained from conversing with the creature in his youth. Just now, however, he opted for a more vague answer.

"I know a bit of them, sir."

His words seemed to have a profound effect on Mr. Ellis. The reverend grasped Max by the free hand and pulled him into the house. The sudden movement upset Bartholomew, sending him into screeching and flapping and the repetitive recitation of two damnable lines of what Max knew to be the mildest part of an even more damnable rhyme.

Miss Farrow blushed again. How interesting. Max would not have guessed her to be the type to own familiarity with the rhyme in question.

His curiosity about Miss Farrow's various knowledge, however, was quickly diverted by Mr. Farrow's barrage of questions.

"Can you help us, sir? Have you experience with this sort of thing? How long do you expect it to take?"

Perhaps if Max had been able to make heads or tails of the man's rambling he could have answered intelligibly. As he could not, and as he had found Miss Farrow's warm brown eyes with their mixture of innocence and admiration to be somewhat of a distraction, Max rather babbled his response.

"I... er, that is..."

Thankfully Bartholomew disrupted things by leaping off his hand and flying up onto the nearby stair rail. He joyfully bobbed his yellow head up and down while he completed the rhyme. Miss Farrow blushed again.

"You can help us, can't you?" Mr. Farrow repeated. "You did come about the advertisement?"

Advertisement? Good gracious, were these people trying to sell the bird? Indeed, he was glad to have arrived when he did. What a disaster it would be if Bartholomew ended up sold off to some stranger. He only hoped he had enough ready blunt to cover the sale. He was hoping not to have need for alerting his solicitor to his arrival in town. Not just yet, at any rate. Not until he knew who could be trusted, and who could not.

"Er, yes. Yes I did come about the advertisement," he replied. "What terms are you suggesting, sir?"

Mr. Farrow beamed and shook his hand excitedly. "Excellent! Thank heavens, sir. Come in, come in. We can make whatever arrangements you see fit, considering the urgent nature of things. Meg, go see if Mrs. Cooper has calmed herself enough to get us some tea. She can bring it to the drawing room."

Mr. Farrow began leading Max toward the doorway where all the hysteria had played out so recently. Max politely removed his hat and followed, giving Miss Farrow a bow and feeling somewhat disappointed to be losing her company already. She, however, appeared in no great hurry to rush off at her father's bidding.

"But Papa—" she began.

Her father shushed her. "Go along, pet. I'm sure Mrs. Cooper is fine. You know she's a durable woman."

"Yes, Papa, but—"

"And perhaps some cakes, if she wouldn't mind," the gentleman added. "Yes, it's a bit early, I think, but tell her some cakes for our guest might be just the thing."

"Of course, Papa, but—"

Mr. Farrow led Max into the drawing room. Miss Farrow followed but he had the distinct impression she would rather not have. Max soon understood why. There, sprawled gracelessly half on and half off the settee was a large woman in bold, matronly garb. It appeared she had at one point been entirely on the settee, but had slid off. Her garb, however, had not. The thick fabric of her gown had remained affixed to the silk of the settee and was now wrapped unceremoniously about her thighs. The effect was not nearly as enticing as a purely verbal description might lead one to think.

Fortunately, the woman appeared to be sleeping and unaware of her dishabille. Unfortunately, the sound of their voices woke her. Her eyes popped open as they entered the room and it was clear she was at first confused by her surroundings. Slowly she took stock of things. She blinked at them and gradually her puffy, blotched face was overcome by an expression of mortification, evidenced by more blotches.

"Good gracious," the surprised reverend said, clearly as mortified to find the woman this way as she was to find herself. "Mrs. Sedley-Stone!"

"Yes, Papa, that's what I meant to remind you," Miss Farrow said, rushing past them to go to the aid of the woman.

Max wasn't at all certain what his response to this vision should be. He knew it would be most improper to stare at the woman whose legs were all but exposed before them, so he looked away. But to look away with so much vigor and enthusiasm might be equally rude. So, rather than turning dramatically around and gouging out his eyes to wipe the image from them, he could only quietly avert his glance in the most gracious, polite fashion possible.

That put his gaze squarely on Miss Farrow's previously noted form. This time it was the backside of her form, to be precise, as she bent in all innocence and Christian charity to help right the older woman's clothes and return her to a more appropriate, seated position. Whether or not it was rude to stare at this Max really did not care. His eyes were not about to re-avert at this point.

"Forgive us, Mrs. Sedley-Stone," the good reverend said in most formal tones. "I cannot express how sorry I am for any discomfort you may have—"

His beautiful apology was interrupted. Bartholomew swooped back into the room and landed directly atop Max's now hatless head. He cringed at the feel of the bird's claws digging into his scalp, while his eyes stung from his hair being brushed down into them. The bird squawked loudly, then most eloquently recited a stanza—in perfect pentameter—declaring what should be done when a woman of dubious morals is found with her skirts up about her this way. It did not involve innocence or Christian charity. Nor did it involve improving the woman's morals. It was, in fact, a line from a song best sung in the company of good friends, aberrant amounts of alcohol, and absolutely no ladies.

None of these conditions were applicable at this time. Both ladies were frozen in stunned disgust. Mrs. Sedley-Stone fell back onto the settee, fainted away. Her turban rolled off onto the floor, but this time her gown stayed where it should be. Miss Farrow sighed, then turned helpless to shrug at Max.

"This happens a lot, I'm afraid," she said.

Mr. Farrow slapped Max on the back. Bartholomew's claws dug in deeper.

"But we have hope now," the older man said brightly. "The Almighty has been gracious, and we have seen our salvation."

Max couldn't quite tell for certain, given that his hair was still down in his eyes and the bird was now turning circles on him which added green and red tail feathers to his visual obstruction, but he got the idea Miss Farrow's expression was not nearly so hopeful as her father's.

"I knew if I advertised, things would work out," the reverend went on. "We needed a parrot trainer, and now here he is. Come, young man. I'll show you up to your room while my daughter handles things down here. You may bring the bird, if you like."

It did not appear as if Max had any choice. Bartholomew was stuck fast to his head and Max could not see to do anything but follow where his new host would lead. So Mr. Farrow needed a parrot trainer, did he? Apparently they were not selling Bartholomew, after all.

Well, this was an interesting turn. Perhaps the old man did have some idea what he was about, after all. No wonder they had put up with the bird's unseemly habits despite the obvious hardship they caused.

Mr. Farrow must know—or at least he must suspect—the same thing that Max did: Bartholomew was the key to a treasure. A treasure, no less, that someone had already killed for. With luck, Max would get the bird to reveal what he knew about both treasure and murder.

Hopefully before the murderer killed again.

About the Author

Susan Gee Heino thinks the sexiest thing a man can do is engage in witty banter. If he happens to be wearing breeches and a cravat while he does this, all the better. If he comes with a noble title, a tortured past, and perhaps even dimples, then he is just about perfect. Her lighthearted Regency Romances are full of quirky heroines who tend to feel exactly the same way—at least they do by the end of the book. Usually it takes a little convincing by the cravat-clad hero. But no matter what adventures ensue, the hero always ends up with his lady. And vice versa.

Ms. Heino lives in rural Ohio with her non-cravat-inclined husband, two very remarkable children, and an accidental collection of critters. She loves to hear from readers so please visit her website or connect on social media.

www. SusanGH.com

Love's funny sometimes!